Wedding Bell Boos

Wedding Bell Boos

A Ravenmist Whodunit
Book Five

BY OLIVIA JAYMES

www.OliviaJaymes.com

Chapter One

THE RAVENMIST INN had been host to many weddings through the years. I'd seen happy brides, sad brides, crying brides, drunk brides, and nightmare brides. I'd seen devoted grooms, cheating grooms, and grooms I wouldn't want to ever see again. But this weekend, the most important wedding of all time was happening.

No, it's not mine. Are you kidding?

Get that thought out of your head. Jack and I haven't been dating all that long and frankly, neither one of us is looking to tie the knot any time soon. Been there, done that. Worn the white dress. It's now shoved in the back of my closet.

The all-important wedding is my best friend Missy's to her long-time boyfriend Dylan. They're just the cutest couple and I think they're going to be really happy together. The inn is hosting the rehearsal dinner tonight and the actual wedding ceremony and reception tomorrow. The renovations to the convention center out in the east pasture were finished just in time. Missy's wedding was going to be the first to be held there.

Did I mention that I'm the maid of honor? And the bachelorette party is tonight after the rehearsal. Consider yourself cordially invited.

Oops. I really should introduce myself, shouldn't I? If we're going to party together, we should be on a first name basis.

My name is Theodosia "Tedi" Hamilton and I'm the proprietor of the Ravenmist Inn in Ravenmist, Illinois. The inn is a rambling old Victorian that's been in my father's family for generations, consists of several acres and seven restored buildings. I'm also the president of the local paranormal society and I'll answer your question before you even have to ask it.

Yes, ghosts are real. As in *really* real. Massively real. Stick around and you'll see for yourself.

"I should check and see how everything is going in the kitchen," I said to Jack as I watched uniformed servers pass silver trays of hors d'oeuvres. The inn's dining room was full of the happy couple's family and friends. "I don't want to run out of food."

Shaking his head, Jack placed his hand on my arm. "When have you ever in the history of the Ravenmist Inn run out of food? No, this is just you not liking that you're not in control. Admit it."

I decided to play dumb.

"Admit what? This is my inn and I have responsibilities."

"Tedi."

"Jack."

With a sigh, he gave me a reproachful look that would have made my mother proud. Where was she anyway?

"Tedi, Missy hired a wedding coordinator so that you

wouldn't have to deal with all the event details this weekend. She wants you to be there for her, remember? She wants you to be able to enjoy this milestone in her life without having to worry if Klaus opened enough wine bottles."

And I wanted to enjoy it with her, be there to support her… But couldn't I be in charge too?

"I may have some control issues," I finally admitted with a groan. "Although I don't think they're that bad."

"They are," he assured me. "Let it go. Is Andrea doing such a terrible job? It looks like everything is fine."

Can we talk about Andrea? Just between you and me?

Because I was beginning to really hate Andrea. She wasn't doing a terrible job. She was doing great. She was so amazingly efficient and always chipper and happy. Smiling. Stress wasn't even a word in her vocabulary. It wasn't normal and I wasn't sure I could trust someone who never needed caffeine.

Wait, I didn't mention that? She doesn't drink coffee. Or tea. Or anything with caffeine. She told me she'd given it up years ago, along with chocolate. I didn't even know how to respond to that. She might not be human, maybe a robot?

She was a nice person, though. A bit strange with her garish wardrobe and bright lipstick. Today she was wearing a fuchsia blouse with sequins around the cuffs and collar.

"Andrea is fine," I replied through gritted teeth. "But she's acting like she runs the inn, not me."

She'd actually shooed me away from the dining room before the guests arrived. All I'd wanted to do was check the table settings and centerpieces. That's it.

I was *shooed*.

"She's running this wedding."

My eyes narrowed dangerously at the man that had taken me to firehouse bingo last Saturday night. He'd bought me a brownie at the snack bar.

"Whose side are you on?"

"Is there a war?"

Clearly, there was. For control, and I had a feeling that I was losing it.

"You're supposed to be on my side."

"I am on your side. But you need to let up on Andrea. She's running the wedding for Missy. You're the maid of honor and Missy's best friend. She wants you with her and not checking on how many roses are in the bouquets."

I opened my mouth to tell him that there better be twelve in mine and twenty-four in Missy's but I didn't get the chance. A booming voice captured my attention from several feet away.

"I can't believe the shoddy arrangements that have been made for this wedding," Vivian said, her loud voice carrying across the crowded room. "It's completely preposterous that they expect us to stay in this rundown roadside motel."

Uh…what? A rundown motel? Those were fightin' words. My family had meticulously cared for this inn for over one hundred and fifty years. It was the finest accommodations in the area, and twice as interesting.

When you add in all the ghosts, that is.

My mother Peggy had also heard Vivian's words and she shot me a look of warning. The same one she'd given me more than a few times before. She wanted me to be nice, and honestly, that's what I wanted too. I didn't want to make trouble for my best friend. Maybe Grand-Aunt Vivian was simply having a bad day.

Okay, let's talk about Vivian. To be precise, she's Dylan's great-aunt, although they didn't see each other much. Missy had never met her until last year because Vivian rarely attended family events.

Vivian was actually Vivian Dashwood, a well-known romance author. From what Missy had told me Vivian lived in a palatial home on the Upper East Side of New York City where she would write her steamy love stories at a large old desk that she swears was once used by Lady Godiva, although it's never been confirmed. I was pretty sure it was just a story.

Great-Aunt Vivian is a colorful character who wears diamonds and evening gowns all day, every day with her perfectly coiffed pale blonde hair. She drinks only champagne after one o'clock and before that she drinks orange juice…with champagne. Basically, she's one completely over the top individual who had an assistant trailing behind her at all times in case she had a great thought or inspiration for her next book.

Missy – and Dylan – had been worrying all week about how we were all going to deal with Great-Aunt Vivian. She was as rich as she was eccentric and wasn't above pulling the inheritance card to get people to bend to her will. Dylan joked that she'd probably leave her entire fortune to her cat just to honk off all of her relatives one last time. He was one of the few that didn't cater to her demands. So no one was more surprised than Missy when she received Vivian's affirmative response to the wedding invitation.

Now here we were.

I slid between Missy and Vivian, which wasn't easy as the older woman was standing far too close for comfort. I gave her my most winning customer service smile. It was better than Andrea's any day of the week.

"I just wanted to let you know that my chef is aware of your dietary concerns and he says that it's no problem."

Vivian looked me right in the eye and scoffed. "I seriously doubt that. I have little to no hope that the dinner will be acceptable, especially after seeing the room I've been given. It's small, cramped, and it smells like mold. The furniture was dusty too. And those canapés have mushrooms in them."

No…they didn't. Unless they crawled in there on their own which I highly doubted.

As for the accommodations, Missy and Dylan had made sure that I had given the best and largest suite to his grandmother. Make no mistake, a family of four could easily stay in that suite and barely see each other.

And there was no dust either. Perish the thought.

I opened my mouth to reply but was elbowed aside by my own mother, who was officiating the wedding. After presiding over the nuptials of two ghosts last year, she'd performed several more weddings and it was now something of a profitable hobby. She'd even asked me to help her build a website to advertise her services.

"Vivian, I'd love to hear about your newest book."

My mother reads thrillers, not romance, but Vivian didn't know that. The older woman looked down her nose at my mother and then seemed to decide that it was a legitimate question.

"I did quite a bit of research for my latest novel. I spent two months in the south of France."

She said the last part with a dramatic wave, her diamonds glinting in the candlelight. Vivian was dressed in lavender silk tonight, a long sweeping gown with a plunging neckline and silver sequins around the waist and hem. She looked fantastic for a woman of a certain age. I should be so lucky. Her hair was piled on top of her head in some sort of complex knot, showing off the dangly earrings that matched the large necklace and bracelet she was wearing.

Vivian Dashwood was literally dripping in diamonds.

A younger woman with large tortoiseshell glasses and brown hair appeared at Vivian's elbow holding a phone. "You have a call from your interior decorator."

Vivian smiled and accepted the phone from the woman. "I'm redoing my home in Martha's Vineyard. Please do excuse me."

"That seemed to make her happy," my mother muttered under her breath. "Too bad they didn't call twenty minutes ago."

"I'm really sorry about Vivian," the other woman apologized. "She's been under a lot of pressure lately because of this deadline. It makes her cranky."

Missy waved away the apology with a big smile. "It's fine. Just fine. We're all a little nervous."

I wasn't nervous. I didn't think my mom was nervous. I was absolutely sure that Jack wasn't nervous.

The young woman held out her hand. "My name is Sadie, by the way. Sadie Holt. I'm Vivian's personal assistant."

Now that was a job that probably didn't pay nearly enough.

Two men elbowed their way through the bodies to sidle up next to Sadie. I recognized both of them from a cookout a few years ago. The older man was Dylan's Uncle Herschel. He was somewhere in his seventies or thereabouts, stiff and formal which I put down to him being an attorney. Technically, he was a great-uncle, but no one seemed to refer to him as such.

The younger man was his son Bandy, who was also an attorney with his father. Bandy was the apple of Herschel's eye and could do no wrong. I'd only met Bandy that one time but he hadn't made that great of an impression. He'd been drunk and more than a little handsy. I'd had to make a point to avoid him. He looked no more sober today than then, his face and especially his nose quite red, guzzling a whiskey from a highball glass.

"Sadie," Herschel's voice boomed. "We need to speak to Vivian immediately. I've left several messages."

Sadie, bless her, didn't bat an eyelash at Herschel's commanding tone, as if he was king of the castle.

"I've given Vivian your message," the woman said in a sweet, patient tone. "She'll get back to you when she has time."

"We need to talk to her now," Bandy said, his own tone not any better than his father's. The younger man was slightly swaying on his feet. "Go tell her."

Sadie simply smiled and shook her head. "You know that's not how this works. No one tells Vivian anything, and she never does anything she doesn't want to. I've given her the message. She'll get back to you in her own time."

It was clear that Sadie's answer wasn't going down well with Herschel and Bandy. The older man had opened up his mouth and looked like he was going into a rant when his youngest son suddenly appeared at his side, smoothly interrupting his father about an important matter that only Herschel himself could deal with.

Alvin. Younger brother to Bandy and, from what I could see from that one meeting, mostly overlooked by his father. Missy had described Alvin as the misfit in the family which I took to mean as a compliment to him. When I'd met him he'd been kind and smiling, and not in the least bit creepy.

Herschel scowled down at Alvin. "I don't have time for this. You deal with it."

Alvin shrugged. "I'm not an attorney, and Aunt Flora says that she's being sued by her dentist. She wants to talk to you, and only you."

Herschel harrumphed, clearly not happy. "Fine, we'll talk to her. Sadie, this is not over. We must speak to Vivian."

Herschel turned on his heel and strode off, Bandy trailing behind him, the whiskey glass still in his hand.

"I'm so sorry Uncle Herschel spoke to you that way," Missy apologized. "Sometimes he can be a little overbearing."

It was Sadie's turn to shrug. "No big deal. He's the least of my daily problems. And he's yelling at the wrong person. Vivian has no intention of speaking with him. She knows what that discussion is about."

Without another word, Sadie also turned and left me, Missy, and my mother Peggy standing there alone. Not that I was complaining.

"What do you think he wants to talk to Vivian about?" I asked. "He seems really upset about it, whatever it is."

Missy sighed and shook her head. "If it's Vivian, then it's money. It's always money."

Dylan jogged up to our group, his face flushed. "Honey, have you seen Zack? I can't find him anywhere."

Zack was Dylan's best friend and best man. He seemed like a nice guy but I hadn't really talked to him because he had a cell phone glued to his ear pretty much twenty-four-seven. I had to wonder whether he could manage to put it away for the ceremony tomorrow. He sure hadn't for the rehearsal tonight. Mom had to practically drag him around by his ear to get him to cooperate.

"I'm guessing he's on the phone," I said. "I can look for him, if you like."

Dylan groaned. "I need to talk to him about holding the

rings. I'll just talk to him later. I'm sure I'll see him. The bachelor party is tonight, after all."

About that bachelor party…Jack was planning to attend.

"Um, what do you all have planned anyway?"

Should we make sure we have bail money? Wait, Jack was the sheriff. He wasn't going to arrest himself.

"I'm not sure," Dylan confessed. "Zack is in charge of it. I told him I wanted something low-key, though. No wild rager or anything."

Frankly, there wasn't much they could get up to in Ravenmist. If they were looking for trouble, they'd have to import it. Even then I couldn't imagine that Jack would be part of any *shenanigans*. Or heaven forbid…*horseplay, nonsense,* and the very worst *hijinks.*

Jack nudged my shoulder, nodding toward the far corner of the dining room.

"I think we have a bigger problem than the bachelor party. Do you see what I see? I think I'd better get us a couple of drinks. We're going to need them."

It took me a moment to understand his cryptic statement, but yes, I did see it. And I couldn't unsee it either.

Vivian. Laughing and flirting with a man.

And that man? Edward, the ghost that lived in Missy's bookstore. My best friend had made it very clear that Dylan's family didn't know about ghosts or how her entire family were supernatural beings. She wanted to keep it that way.

I needed two aspirin and a Caribbean vacation. Stat.

Chapter Two

"**O**H MY STARS, Vivian is talking to Edward. He's not supposed to be here. He's supposed to be at the bookstore." Missy pressed her hands against her cheeks. "This cannot be happening. If I close my eyes, and then open them it will all be gone."

My friend wasn't going to be that lucky. She wasn't seeing things. Vivian and Edward were having the time of their lives. Or her life...since Edward was...you know...dead.

"She is happy," I said, watching the couple laugh and smile. "That's something. Can I say that I'm surprised you trusted Edward with the bookstore? I thought he was only doing inventory for you."

Missy shrugged. "No one wanted to work today. I figured he could be trusted to run the cash register. He's very tech savvy."

That was true. Edward loved technology.

"I hope he locked the door behind him when he left the bookstore."

Although I couldn't imagine anyone going in and stealing from Missy. It wasn't Ravenmist's style.

"He better have or I'll fire him."

Those words surprised me and I put them down to stress. Missy had never fired anyone for anything. She was far too nice.

"Are you going to go over there and tell him to get back to work?"

Missy took a step and then hesitated. "I should but…Vivian actually does look happy for the first time. I just want everyone to be happy and enjoy themselves this weekend. She's making me crazy, Tedi. She hates everything. I think she hates me."

"No one could possibly hate you. I only met her at check-in but she seems like a real snot. Just ignore her. Dylan doesn't care about the inheritance, right?"

"Not at all."

"Then ignore her. She has no power over you and Dylan."

"It's easy for you to say. You don't have Dylan's mom and dad hovering around and wanting us to make sure Vivian is satisfied."

"Trust me when I say that woman will never be satisfied. I've seen her type before. Don't waste your energy."

"I just want everything to be perfect."

Ah, the bane of every wedding. Perfection. I'd done it too, although I'm not proud of it. Eventually, my mother had pulled me aside and told me that the point of the day was to get married. If the cake didn't show up, I'd still be married. It sort of shook me out of my bride-induced stupor and back to the real world. Familial pressure is a real thing, and poor Missy was as susceptible as the next person.

"No such thing," I replied briskly. "And it doesn't matter anyway. This is your weekend, not Vivian's. You and Dylan are more important than some grouchy old writer."

Missy heaved a sigh of relief. "I love it when you sound so sure of yourself."

"I've never been so sure. Forget her. Let Edward entertain her. She'll never figure out that he's a ghost."

Jack had slipped off to the bar and was now joining me again, this time with a glass of champagne in each hand. He gave one to me which I accepted gratefully before nodding toward the odd couple in the dining room.

"Should we separate them?"

"There's no way she'll figure out that he's a ghost. Especially when he's this close to me. He looks completely human and alive."

Ahem. I may have forgotten to mention that my escort this evening was a demon. A *good* demon. He'd moved to Ravenmist to protect us in the ongoing, centuries-old battle between good and evil. So far, he was doing a great job.

As an extremely powerful demon, Jack exuded some off the charts energy to the town and that had somehow given the spirits almost a "new lease on life", so to speak. They appeared to be alive and kicking aside from being rather pale.

Jack handed the other glass of champagne to my friend. "Missy, you better get back out there and help your husband-to-be. I think Dylan is ready to flee the state and change his name."

Missy groaned and rubbed her temples. "What happened?

He was perfectly fine when I left him at the table."

"His cousin found him. Something about investing in a sure thing. I assume that it's anything but sure."

That was Jack in a nutshell. Blunt.

"Bandy has had many get rich quick schemes over the years," Missy admitted. "He's always trying to get others to invest their money."

"I tried to help him but he whispered that I should save myself and make a run for it."

"So you did?" I asked with a grin. "I've never seen you run from a challenge, Jack."

"And I hope I never do, but I thought that maybe he'd accept help from Missy if he wouldn't take it from me."

"I better get back there," Missy said with another heavy sigh. "Bandy can make me the bad guy when Dylan tells him no."

Missy flew back down the hall, leaving Jack and I.

"Dylan's family dynamics are a mess," Jack said with a scowl. "Vivian is a nightmare. I can't believe they just take the abuse and go back for more. And the uncle and cousin aren't much better."

"I'll just be honest. From what Dylan has said, the old battle axe is loaded. Rolling in dough. She uses the threat of writing them out of her will to keep everyone in line."

"Charming."

"That's what I thought too."

Andrea, the wedding coordinator, was flitting around the dining room and stopped to speak to us. Her sequined blouse glittered in the candlelight.

"Tedi, I just have to tell you that your chef is such a sweet-heart. He's so wonderful."

Whatever Andrea had Klaus doing, I was going to hear about later.

"He is terrific."

The other woman's smile widened, showing off a mouthful of whiter than white teeth. They were probably that bright because she didn't drink any caffeine or eat chocolate.

"He's more than that. He's a genius. And so cooperative. I just gave him a list of Ms. Dashwood's dinner requests and he said it was no problem. So helpful."

Yep, I was definitely going to hear about that.

"If you need me to talk to him—"

"No, it's all fine." Andrea waved away my concerns. "Everything is under control. You can just sit back and relax. Enjoy your weekend off. Lucky you."

Lucky me.

Andrea headed toward Missy and Dylan, practically dancing in her high heels. She was just that gosh darn happy.

"Tedi…"

Jack had a *tone*.

"What? I didn't say anything. I was nice. I offered to help."

"Seriously, you need to relax. Andrea's on top of things. Just let it go."

I could absolutely let it go. No problem.

But maybe I should dash back to the kitchen and make sure.

You know…just in case.

LATER THAT EVENING, the bachelorette party was in full swing on the back patio of the inn. Daisy – the owner of the town cafe The Grateful Raven – had brought a karaoke machine and currently my mother was blasting out a fantastic rendition of "Stand By Your Man". It was an ironic choice because she'd been divorcing my dad for over a year now. They didn't seem to be in any hurry about it either, telling me that these sorts of things were complicated.

It was a lovely early summer night on the plains of Illinois. Not too hot, not too chilly. Even the bugs were staying away thanks to the lit tiki torches placed strategically around the back deck. There was a table of finger foods and sweets, provided by Daisy, along with a full bar provided by me. Luckily, we didn't have a party animal in the bunch and everyone had held onto their dignity. So far.

Missy had sworn up and down that she didn't want a wild soiree with loud music, drunk guests, and questionable party favors. She simply wanted to hang out with her friends on her last night of being single, listen to some music, and eat food that wasn't good for her. I had her covered. My own bachelorette party was so low-key we were almost asleep by ten o'clock.

Although Andrea wasn't in charge of this get-together, she was somehow still here, flitting around the food buffet and the drinks bar as if she was the hostess. It was Daisy, my mom, and myself who were hosting this little shindig and I wasn't sure why Andrea was even here. Didn't she have things to do for the wedding tomorrow? Knowing Missy, though, she'd probably invited the wedding coordinator. That was completely fine, but it didn't mean she needed to monitor how the food was holding out.

Crabby. That's how I was acting. It wasn't hurting anyone that Andrea was here. Jack was right – and I hate it when he is – but I needed to cut Andrea some slack. She was a nice, hard-working person who was just trying to do a good job and earn a living. I was making this all about me and frankly, that's not a good look. I vowed to be a heck of a lot nicer. She was doing a great job. Even if it wasn't exactly how I would have done it.

I had found a comfortable seat, a slice of pie, and a strawberry daiquiri to make me happy while I watched some of the women dance or chat with each other. It was a casual, happy gathering and I was glad to see that Missy was enjoying herself.

"Are you going to sing too?" Missy asked, dragging herself away from the karaoke. Daisy had cued up "I Am Woman" by Helen Reddy and was launching herself into the song with gusto. She had a decent voice too.

"I don't think anyone wants that," I replied. "You know I can't carry a tune in a bucket."

Normally I *mouthed* the words to the happy birthday song. I couldn't sing a lick, and I wasn't planning on imbibing enough alcohol tonight for me to forget that fact.

Which I had a few times in the past. Luckily, there isn't any video evidence of this or I'd have to move away and join the French Foreign Legion.

"You're not that bad," Missy protested, but in a half-hearted way. She knew how badly I sang, but she was so nice she couldn't just say it.

The sad thing was that I loved music and would often sing loudly in the shower where the only person that could hear me was Terrence, the ghost that lived in my closet. Eventually, he'd asked me to stop singing. Even dead he didn't want to hear me.

"I am that bad. I'm going to stay far away from that karaoke machine." I nodded toward Andrea who was currently chatting with my mother. "I see that you invited Andrea. That was nice."

Missy and I had known each other since kindergarten. She wasn't fooled for a second.

"She's doing an amazing job. I just wanted you to be able to have fun this weekend."

"I didn't say a word."

"You didn't have to. It was Alvin who actually recommended Andrea. I think he said that he met her at a book club meeting or something like that. She's done work for him several times and has done an excellent job. I have to say she's been terrific so far this weekend."

"She has been. And I am having fun so...thank you."

Missy pointed to the double doors leading into the dining room. "If you're bound and determined to worry about something, forget about Andrea and the wedding. I'd be worrying about that."

I had to sit up and crane my neck at a forty-five-degree angle, but I finally saw the *that* Missy was referring to. Vivian wasn't in attendance at the bachelorette party.

She and Edward – the ghost – were sitting in my bar chatting like old friends. I had to wonder if she'd noticed that Edward hadn't eaten or had any drinks. He was a ghost, after all. Would she notice that he wasn't breathing either?

Standing, I walked over to the double doors and peered inside. From that vantage point, I could see into the bar where Vivian was sitting across from Edward. Missy joined me, our noses almost pressed against the glass. "What do you think they're talking about anyway?"

"Edward loves books so I would imagine that's what they're talking about."

"Has he read her?"

"Maybe. If not, I bet he will now. They seem to really like each other and can I say, thank goodness, because he's keeping her busy, happy, and occupied. It's been far more pleasant in the last few hours."

Out of the corner of my eye, I saw Zack coming down the stairs with Uncle Herschel. They, in contrast to Vivian and Edward, did not look like they were enjoying each other's company. Zack was scowling and Herschel looked furious.

"Dare I ask what they're talking about?"

"I have no idea but I don't think it's a pleasant conversation."

Just then, Herschel raised his fist at Zack as if he was going to take a swing. Zack just laughed, knocking the older man's hand to the side before striding away toward the doors where Missy and I were standing. We stepped back, casually pretending that we hadn't been spying.

Zack pushed open the doors and headed straight for Andrea in the corner. We couldn't hear what they were saying because they were both whispering but it was a brief conversation. After a few minutes Zack turned and left, waving at Missy and I as he headed inside.

"That was weird. What would Zack have to talk to Andrea about?"

Missy gave me a strange look. "I'm not worried about Zack and Andrea. He's probably just delivering a message from Dylan. I'm more concerned about him and Uncle Herschel. I think I'm going to just stay out of it, though. Hopefully, it will all blow over. I don't want them to get physical at my wedding tomorrow."

Tomorrow. The wedding. The Big Day.

"So are you ready? Are you nervous? Dylan's a great guy."

Missy glanced over her shoulder before answering. "I am nervous but not about marrying Dylan. I know that's the right thing to do. I'm worried someone in my jurisdiction is going to buy the farm during the wedding and I'll turn into a reaper right at the altar. Dylan's family doesn't know about me. Or the ghosts in town either."

That thought had occurred to me these last months as the

date had grown ever closer.

"Honestly, what are the chances? Remote at best. Everyone in town will be at the wedding. It will be fine."

"Grandma tried a spell to change the reaper to my cousin for the day but we have no idea if it actually worked. Unless…you know…"

"Let's hope no one dies tomorrow. Seriously, it will be fine. You and Dylan are going to get married and it's going to be a smooth day. Nothing strange is going to happen."

Probably. Hopefully.

Honestly, what were the odds?

Chapter Three

"WOW, THAT'S…PINK."

Jack and I were sitting in my apartment early the next morning eating a bite of breakfast before all of the festivities. I wouldn't get a chance to see much of him most of the day so he'd stopped by to visit for a few minutes and chat. He was on duty today until one, when he'd head home to take a quick shower and change into his suit for the ceremony and reception. The wedding started precisely at two-thirty. Missy was adamant that she would walk down the aisle on the upsweep of the clock.

The bride would be arriving in less than an hour to get ready, and I'd taken my maid of honor dress out of the garment bag last night and hung it on my bedroom door so it could air out. I didn't want to smell like a plastic bag when I walked down the aisle.

"It's rose-colored."

"Tedi, it's the color of bubblegum."

I shot Jack a nasty look and fluffed the tulle skirt a little. "It is not."

"It is too. It looks exactly like the color of gum that I had when I was a kid. I could blow humungous bubbles with it."

"Why are you being so argumentative?"

Jack was so gosh darn stubborn. He'd argue about the color of the sky if you'd let him.

"I'm not being argumentative." He lifted up his hands in a sign of surrender. "I'm simply making an observation. The dress is very pink."

"It's Missy's choice," I said defensively. "I would have chosen another color but she's always dreamed about having a pink wedding."

"Then she got her wish."

"I want Missy to have her dream wedding, no matter what it takes." I shook my finger at him. "And I don't want to hear any of your cynical talk today. Missy's really happy and she loves Dylan. We're going to be supportive if it kills us. I know that we're old and cynical but for one day we're going to smile and pretend that getting married is the most wonderful thing in the world."

"I'm supportive. I couldn't be more supportive. I'm thrilled when other people get married."

"What was your wedding like?" I asked Jack, who was now lounging on my couch after sucking up scrambled eggs, bacon, and toast that I'd made with my own two hands. I didn't want to bother my chef with cooking me breakfast when he had so much to do today.

"It was not pink."

This man was a menace.

"I assumed it wasn't, although I wouldn't mind seeing you in a pink tie and cummerbund."

"It was small. Less than thirty people. If there was a color theme, I don't remember it."

"Don't give Missy any trouble about the pink," I warned him. "She loves it and we're not going to ruin her day by being divorced pessimists."

I am an optimist. I'd been working on that for almost a year now.

"I wouldn't dream of it." His expression softened. "Seriously, I would never ruin Missy's day just because I'm a grouch about marriage. I want her and Dylan to be happy."

"Good." I gave him some serious side eye. "Were you this cynical on your wedding day?"

He barked with laughter. "I was not born a pessimist, Tedi. But between law enforcement and getting a divorce, I guess you could say that I grew into one. What's your excuse?"

"I think I was born cynical and sarcastic," I admitted. "I think I've always been this way. Isn't that sad?"

"Are you telling me that you weren't at least a little starry-eyed on your wedding day? I wouldn't believe that. You believed in ghosts long before you ever saw one. I think that's pretty optimistic."

He had a point. Maybe I wasn't a total cynical loss after all. There was a rainbow in those gray clouds.

"I did think that I was going to live happily ever after," I said with a sigh. "I thought that all the way up to the time he told me he wanted to find himself."

Jack would never tell anyone that because he wouldn't want to admit that he'd *lost* anything, ever.

"Did he? Find himself?"

"He found himself in as many women's beds as possible, so I guess so. At the rate he's going through eligible females he may have to relocate to another major metropolitan area."

It was his turn to give some side eye. "Does it bother you?"

Jealousy didn't seem like Jack's style.

"No. Let me say that again. No. Not a bit. Has your ex dated much?"

Jack was in one of his rare talkative moods. I wasn't going to let this chance pass me by to learn a little more about him.

"I'm not sure. I know she's dated because Tyler will talk about them when he meets them, but I don't have any idea of how often she dates or if she's had any serious relationships. And Tedi, I know what you're doing. If there's something you want to know about me, just ask. You don't have to sneak around a subject to get me to answer."

Actually, I did.

"You say to ask and when I do, you somehow manage to not answer and change the subject."

He grinned and took a drink from his coffee cup. "That sounds like me."

"So asking you doesn't work," I pointed out.

"If you ask me a question that I think you should know the answer to, I'll answer it."

Which meant that the questions he didn't think I needed to know...

A chill of cold air ran over me and then Terrence, my closet ghost, appeared in front of us. He had his arms crossed over his chest and was wearing a sour expression, which sort of surprised me. He was generally a pretty happy and easygoing spirit. He didn't have many worries...being dead and all.

"When is she leaving?" he said in a demanding tone, which was also not like him at all. "I don't think that I like her. She's not very nice."

I didn't have a clue who Terrence was talking about. He liked to mingle among the guests but he didn't speak to them usually unless they talked to him first.

"When is who leaving?" Jack asked. He and Terrence had become close friends the last few months. "Who's not nice?"

"That woman," Terrence moaned dramatically. "She's completely monopolizing Edward. He and I were supposed to play video games last night but he was *too busy*. Now he's told me that he's not going to sit with me at the reception because he has a date to the wedding."

I knew exactly who he was talking about.

"Vivian Dashwood," I replied. "She's Dylan's great-aunt. Apparently, she and Edward have taken quite a liking to one another."

It looked like Edward was the type to dump all of his friends when he met a woman. I wouldn't have thought that of him, but you never know about people. After all, Vivian thought she was being escorted to the wedding by a much younger man when in actuality he was far older than she was. Or I think so. I'd have to do the math and frankly, I hate math. They might be around the same age.

"She'll be gone tomorrow," Jack said in a soothing tone. "Then everything will go back to normal. And you can sit with me at the ceremony and reception. With Tedi in the wedding party, I'll be on my own quite a bit today."

Jack was the sheriff in this town and loved by pretty much everyone except the criminals. He would never be alone or bored unless he wanted to be, but I thought he was being super sweet to take care of Terrence like that. He was a sensitive spirit and Edward wasn't always the nicest of friends. They had a blow up like this every couple of months or so.

"Won't Tyler be with you?" Terrence asked, already looking happier than he had a few moments ago.

"He's at his mom's in Chicago for a few weeks."

Tyler was a wonderful young man and since coming to Ravenmist had blossomed more than anyone could have imagined. He was deeply involved with the drama club in addition to the paranormal society, and he'd been in a play this spring. He'd done an amazing job. Jack wasn't so sure, however, that he wanted his son to be an actor, but he'd wisely kept his mouth shut.

Terrence grinned, his former mood just a memory. "Thanks, Jack. That would be great."

Now that his jovial nature was restored, I had to remind him of our deal.

"Remember that you're going to make yourself scarce today," I said. "Missy and the other ladies will be showing up here soon to get dressed."

Missy's family wouldn't be shocked to see a ghost but the bride had asked for a strictly girl's day. I think she'd assumed that Terrence would hang out with Edward.

"No problem. I can go visit Charles and Amelia today."

Charles and Amelia were two recently married ghosts who lived above the diner. Both Terrence and Charles loved modern technology, especially playing video games.

"I appreciate your flexibility, Terrence. Thank you."

"You're welcome, Tedi. See you later."

With another wave of chill and a soft pop, Terrence was gone again.

"What are we going to do about Vivian and Edward?" I asked Jack when we were alone again.

He shrugged. "What can we do? And why would we do it?"

"Because he's a ghost and she might notice how he's not breathing?"

"If she hasn't noticed by now, then she probably won't ever notice. And if she has noticed but has bought into the delusion that all the spirits around here are alive, then we don't have a problem either. Let's face it, most of the residents of Ravenmist are under a mass delusion that these ghosts are alive and kicking. Who are we to ruin it for them? They're happy. Don't you want Vivian happy? It will make Missy's day a lot easier."

I did want Vivian happy. I wanted Missy to be happy even more. I just didn't want Vivian – or anyone else for that matter – to figure out that some of the guests weren't actually alive. That might certainly put a damper on the occasion.

I had to cross my fingers and hope everything went smoothly today. Keep telling myself that it would all be fine. Peachy. Awesome. Great.

I could almost feel the optimism surging in my veins.

Missy and Dylan were going to have the perfect wedding.

THE CEREMONY WAS beautiful. Truly mushy and heartfelt, and I – true cynic that I am – cried through the whole thing. It was so lovely to see Missy and Dylan finally tying the knot. I could easily see that they loved each other and it certainly restored my faith in relationships to see two people so perfect together. Maybe…someday…I might get married again.

Now the reception was in full swing. We'd eaten dinner, made toasts, and Missy and Dylan had danced their first dance as a married couple. My maid of honor toast must have been pretty decent because Missy had been misty-eyed at the end of it. We'd hugged and I'd choked up as well. She was the *bestest* best friend in the world, and I was so lucky to have her in my life. Especially since I was a sarcastic pessimist and she was a sunny optimist. Which couldn't be easy when she was a Grim Reaper for a living.

Jack and I had taken a few turns on the dance floor and I had to say that he was a darn fine dancer as long as we didn't try anything too complicated. I had rhythm but I wasn't always the most graceful, so we kept it simple.

On the opposite side of the room, Vivian and Edward had spent most of the reception laughing and talking loudly. Vivian was clearly getting drunk, so perhaps she didn't notice that Edward wasn't drinking anything. When she wasn't looking, I assumed he was pouring his champagne into the nearest potted plant.

Note to self. When those plants inevitably die, send bill to Edward.

Terrence, Charles, and Amelia were having a grand time and because Jack was in such close proximity not one person was going to be able to tell that they were ghosts. They looked positively glowing with life.

But the best part of the reception was yet to come. I was looking forward to the cutting of the cake because...cake. Missy and Dylan had chosen a vanilla with a dark chocolate ganache filling. I was practically salivating over it every time I walked by. I could smell the delicious aroma of sugar from the dance floor. Jack wasn't particularly fond of cake and he'd said I could have his slice in addition to my own. It wasn't an offer I was going to forget.

Jack handed me a fresh glass of champagne after we'd exited the dance floor and took our seats. I was content to watch the other dancers, especially Daisy, who was really good. She had some major moves and a new boyfriend to boogie with.

"Look at Daisy," I said to Jack. "I wish I was half that good. She's amazing."

"Your mother is no slouch either." Jack nodded toward where my mother was…gasp…dancing with my father. They looked good together. "Your mom and your dad know their way around the dance floor."

"They took dance lessons for their wedding."

As the song ended, Andrea stood at the microphone and announced it was time to throw the bouquet. I had to admit that she'd done an excellent job today. I'd barely seen her for most of the reception but I couldn't miss her when she was around. Today she was wearing a sleeveless cotton sweater in a neon green shade with yellow feathers around the neckline. *Feathers.* It was a bold fashion choice. And bright too.

The single women were beginning to gather at one end of the dance floor with Missy several feet away, ready to toss her bouquet of roses. I wasn't surprised when my own mother took her place among them, even though she and my dad had spent most of the reception together.

Andrea jogged up to my table, wearing a huge smile. "You too, Tedi."

Me too, what? Jack was clearing his throat and obviously trying not to laugh out loud. I couldn't think of anything that I'd done that was even remotely funny unless you count me wearing this pink dress. Missy thought I looked great and that's all I cared about.

Jack nudged me with his elbow. "She wants you to go out there for the flower toss."

Oh heck no.

But Andrea was grinning, showing off all those white teeth again. She was a dentist's dream.

"Yes, Tedi. All the single women need to be out on the dance floor."

I didn't think this sort of thing was required. I was about to graciously decline when Missy came over to see what was going on.

"I was just getting your maid of honor to join the group," Andrea said, clapping her hands together encouragingly. "Then we'll be ready to have you toss the bouquet."

"C'mon, Tedi," Missy said. "We can't cut the cake until we do this."

Apparently, my mother had decided to join in on this little party. She stood over me, her hands on her hips wearing a disapproving expression.

"You don't want to disappoint your best friend, do you?" Peggy asked. "You're the maid of honor. You have to participate."

Three sets of eyes stared back at me, including the one set that I truly didn't want to disappoint – Missy. If she wanted me to stand in that gaggle of desperate single women then I would. I'd just strategically move out of the way when the time came. There was no way I wanted that bouquet.

"Fine." I stood and smoothed down my pink tulle skirt.

"Excuse me, Jack. I'll be right back."

"Take your time. Have fun."

I was really going to get revenge for that grin he was wearing. Wait…don't they have a garter toss too? He needed to do that.

I gathered with the other single women, positioning myself close to the back of the crowd. Missy's bouquet was quite heavy so I hoped she'd just chuck it to the first row and then I could go sit down. Missy's cousin Emily was prowling the front of the group like a wrestler, knees bent in a "ready" position. She'd been dating her boyfriend for over five years and he had yet to pop the question. Having met him, I wasn't sure why she was still with him, but you never know what goes on between two people. I was happy to let her have it but then Missy looked over her shoulder at us and beckoned me to come closer.

"Move up, Tedi. You'll never catch it from there."

That was pretty much the point.

My mother appeared at my elbow and gave me a wink. "I guess I should let the younger ladies have it."

"If you want it, Mom, go for it. You have just as much right to it."

"What about you, sweetheart? Don't you want it?"

"No, I do not."

Mom glanced over at Jack who was still grinning ear to ear. "Love comes when you least expect it."

So does the flu.

Missy had her back to us, and Andrea was at the microphone counting down from five.

Five, four, three, two…one!

The bouquet sailed into the air, and I stepped back, not wanting to be in anyone's way. Emily made an acrobatic leap into the air but somehow it all went awry. She twisted her body toward the flying object but she must have had far too much momentum – and excitement – behind her. There was an audible gasp from the crowd as she did a barrel roll in the air and fell against the gift table located in front of the coat room, the wrapped boxes scattering. The gift table lurched against the set of double doors, the doors flew open, and Emily fell to the ground in a heap, with the bouquet landing in my mother's arms.

Needless to say, all the guests were in an uproar. Jack was the first to jump to his feet, and as a first responder, he assessed Emily's injuries as best he could. Someone yelled out that they were calling 911, although Emily appeared to be dazed but conscious. Jack was having her move her limbs slowly to see if anything was broken. Even if she hadn't, she was definitely going to be black and blue from that martial arts move she'd made.

I was filling a glass with cool water to hand to Jack so he could give it to Emily when my mother tugged on my sleeve.

"Tedi, we have a problem."

"I know. I hope Emily is okay."

"A *bigger* problem, Tedi."

My mother had a strange expression on her face, almost like she was about to be sick. She'd turned a rather unattractive shade of green and I didn't think it was from the scent of the roses she now held in her arms.

She tugged on my arm again and had me following her around the rectangular table and into the coat room. Because it was a warm day, it had gone unused and was currently storing extra chairs.

When I stepped in she pointed to our "bigger problem" but she hadn't needed to. I could see what it was right in front of me. Suddenly, I understood why she was nauseous. The sight before me wasn't pretty.

Vivian. Lying on my brand-new ceramic tile in a bright red pool of blood.

With a gigantic gash in the back of her head. She wasn't moving either.

Had Vivian been murdered? I needed to get Jack in here. Pronto.

Chapter Four

MURDER MADE JACK surly. He hated asparagus and the texture of bananas, but he hated homicide a million times more. Especially if it was in his town. That was a major pet peeve. So needless to say, he was none too happy about Vivian Dashwood's violent demise.

Frankly, I was less worried about Jack's foul mood than what this had done to my best friend and her brand-new husband. This was their wedding day. It was supposed to be one of the happiest days of their lives and now they had a corpse with a chalk outline ruining the fun. I guess it would certainly be *memorable*.

Can I also say that Missy's grandmother had done a great job with the spell, because at no time did my best friend turn from a radiant bride in a flowing white dress into a black garbed Grim Reaper with a scythe. As they'd hoped, her cousin had transformed but luckily no one was looking at him as everyone's attention was on the bouquet toss.

Jack's deputies had arrived and cordoned off the coat room. The state forensic unit was on its way to look for evidence, but in the meantime the crime scene needed to be preserved as much as possible. The coroner was in the room with Jack to examine the body and pronounce the death. Only then was anyone else allowed to touch the body.

"She's dead," Dr. Myron Douglas bellowed so loudly I was sure they could hear at the main inn. "From the body temperature probably less than an hour ago."

Myron was about a hundred and fifty-five years old, give or take a decade, and his hearing wasn't what it used to be.

"Looks like it was a blunt instrument to the back of the head," he shouted so all the guests could hear. "She probably didn't see it coming."

Wearing a pair of rubber gloves, Jack lifted a heavy wooden bookend in the shape of a lion from the floor near the body. It was smeared with blood. "She was probably hit with this."

I knew that bookend well. It used to reside in the drawing room at the main building, but I'd changed out the decorations a few months ago and stored it in the supply closet here at the convention center along with a few other pieces. I'd thought that perhaps I might use them eventually in the foyer but had never gotten around to doing anything with them. I'd never liked that lion bookend set, to be honest.

"Tedi, we have a problem."

Missy had somehow snuck up on me. I should have been paying more attention to her than to Jack's investigation. What kind of friend was I? The bad kind.

Giving Missy all of my attention, I placed my arm around

her shoulders. "I know. I wish I could rewind time so that this didn't happen at your wedding. I just wanted this day to be perfect for you."

Rolling her eyes, Missy groaned. "Not this problem. A *new* problem."

How many problems could we have today? Emily had already been loaded into an ambulance and taken to the county hospital so they could x-ray her ankle and wrist. She was not a happy camper either. My mother had given her the bouquet of flowers as a friendly gesture and Emily had snarled at her as she'd accepted them.

"I'm afraid to ask what the new problem is."

"Follow me to the ladies' room."

Doing as I was told, I followed Missy to the ladies' room where I found Daisy, my mother, and Missy's grandmother Lane.

And Vivian. Boy-howdy, was she mad. Like wet hen mad. I'd never actually seen red cheeks on a ghost before but she had them. She was stomping around the bathroom so hard I could hear the echoes bounce off the tile walls.

My mother sighed, her brows comically raised. "As you can see, we have an issue here."

"Vivian won't go into the light," Daisy added. "She doesn't believe she's dead."

"Has she looked into a mirror?" I asked. "Because she'll see that she's...you know."

Vivian stopped pacing around long enough to turn on me. "I

am not dead. If I were dead, I would know it. This is some bizarre practical joke and I don't find it funny at all. These women won't let me go back to the reception."

Because we couldn't have a newly minted spirit prancing about while their body was lying on the coatroom floor growing cold. That would definitely scare the guests. At least Dylan's side of the family. Missy's kin wouldn't bat an eye.

"This is no joke," Daisy protested. "Trust me when I say that you're dead."

Vivian turned her wrath onto Missy. "What kind of sick, twisted practical joke is this? You people need therapy."

Missy's grandmother Lane hadn't spoken yet. She'd been quietly watching all of this unfold before stepping forward.

"If I can prove that you're dead, will you believe me?"

Vivian stopped stomping and gave all of her attention to Lane. "How can you do that?"

"I can cast a spell that will allow us to walk through the reception without being seen by anyone. Then you can see with your own eyes that you're lying dead in the coatroom."

We'd be invisible? Cool. Where do I sign up? This could come in handy.

Vivian's chin lifted in challenge. "A spell? I'm supposed to believe that?"

Lane raised her arms, palms up and blue fire sparked from her fingers.

"Yes, you are."

"Fine," Vivian acquiesced, eyeing those blue flames suspiciously. "Show me my dead body. If you really can."

Lane began to chant, words that I didn't understand, and the lights flickered in the bathroom before going dark altogether. I grabbed onto the tile wall for support because I suddenly felt like I was on a ride at the county fair, tilting in one direction for a few seconds before turning in the opposite a second later. The lights flickered again and then came on. We were all standing in exactly the same spot we were before as if nothing had happened.

Lane opened the bathroom door. "We can go out there now."

My mother hesitated, her gaze darting around the room. "Wait…how do you know that it worked? What if they see us?"

Peggy had asked the exact question floating around in my head. A few words and they were invisible? This was absolutely a spell I needed to learn.

"Trust me," Lane said, holding the door open wider. "Vivian, I warn you that the crime scene isn't a pretty sight."

Vivian wore a dubious expression but followed Missy's grandmother from the bathroom, all of us at her heels. The guests were all milling around the double doors to the coatroom, and just as Lane had said, no one seemed to notice us. Even Missy, the actual bride in a huge white dress, didn't catch anyone's attention.

We were, indeed, invisible. This was so awesome.

I flapped my arms and twirled in a circle. No one batted an eye.

Except for my mother who rolled hers and then shook her

head.

"You have to admit that this is cool," I said. "C'mon, this could be very useful."

Peggy sighed and then smiled. "You do have a point. I would have loved this back in college. I think my roommate was telling stories about me behind my back."

Lane cleared her throat and then motioned for us to continue into the coatroom.

"Vivian, I think you'll see that we're telling you the truth."

Lane was correct. It wasn't a pretty sight, and I'd already seen it once. This time wasn't any better. There was a huge pool of blood on my tile floor and Vivian was still lying in it, although now she was face up. Today's evening gown had been a pale peach color with gold buttons on the bodice but now it was stained a reddish-brown. The doctor wasn't anywhere that I could see but Jack was still standing by the body, telling his deputies to keep the guests out of his crime scene. He sounded frustrated which wasn't a surprise. Did I mention that he hates murder in his town?

Vivian stepped forward to examine herself more closely. We all heard her gasp and then she made a choking sound as if she might be physically ill. Could ghosts puke? I had a feeling I might find out.

"I'm dead. I'm really dead."

Poor Vivian's voice was soft and sad. I felt terrible for her; finding out you're dead couldn't be an easy thing. Missy had said that a good portion of her clients fought the idea of death but seeing it play out like this was heartbreaking. While Vivian wasn't super young, she'd been in good health and probably had lots of plans for her future. It was all ruined now.

Vivian turned to Missy. "Who did this to me? Who killed me?"

Before Missy could answer, Herschel barreled into the room with two deputies right behind him, trying to pull him back.

"Someone needs to tell us what's going on here," Herschel said, his tone huffy. "We've been waiting out there a long time. Are you in charge?"

Straightening up to his full height of six-two, Jack nodded. "I am in charge here and you're walking all over our crime scene. I need to ask you to step back into the reception room immediately."

Instead of waiting for the older man's response, Jack began walking toward him, getting into his personal space so that Herschel only had two options. One, he could walk backward out of the coatroom, or two, allow Jack to physically run into him.

He chose the former. Smart.

Bandy was waiting for him just outside the door, drink in hand. His red face told me that he was inebriated. That and the way he was clutching a chair to stay upright.

"We're the next of kin," Herschel announced. "I didn't give permission for any of this."

Jack wasn't taking any guff today.

"This is a criminal investigation," Jack shot back, his eyes narrowed dangerously. Herschel's throat bobbed visibly. "I don't need your permission. What I need for you to do is stay out of my way. If you don't, I will arrest you for obstructing justice. Am I being clear?"

Herschel didn't answer, only nodding and taking another step back. Bandy, still swaying on his feet, lifted his half-empty glass. "Here's to the old bat. Life sure is brighter with her gone."

"No one's going to miss her," Herschel muttered under his breath, but he didn't realize that I was standing close enough to hear.

In fact, our entire group was close enough to hear, including Vivian. She didn't look happy at all. She started walking among the guests and listening to their conversations. From her expression, I had the terrible feeling that they weren't lamenting her recent passing.

"This is awful," I whispered to my mother. "We need to get her out of here. Listening to all these people be happy that she's dead cannot be good for her."

"Let's get her back into the bathroom," Daisy suggested. "We can try and convince her again to go into the light."

Lane herded us toward the ladies' room. "The spell won't last forever."

Glancing over my shoulder, I looked right into Jack's eyes. He was standing only a few feet away and the intensity of his stare gave me a jolt. There was no maybe here. He definitely saw me. I could tell. Could demons see through spells?

Back in the ladies' room, Lane and Missy were trying to

convince Vivian to go into the light.

"You don't want to be in the in-between," Missy said. "You deserve your eternal rest."

Assuming that's the way Vivian was going...

"I can't believe this," Vivian lamented. "They all don't care that I'm dead. Only Alvin cares. He was truly sad."

I'd seen Alvin earlier and he did appear to be genuinely upset about his great-aunt.

My mother nudged my elbow. "Should we tell her that she was difficult in life? I'm not sure if it would make her better or worse."

"Probably worse, Mom. Because there's nothing she can do about it now."

A chill ran over my arms, raising goosebumps and then there was a pop in the air. Just like that, Edward was standing in the middle of our circle, his brows pulled together and his lips a thin line.

"Don't listen to them, Viv. Don't listen to a word that they say. You don't have to cross over. They just want you to so that they can get their quarterly bonus. We're just numbers to them."

Vivian threw open her arms and hugged Edward; an audible buzz sounded when they touched. "Eddie, I'm so glad that you're here. I'm dead. Did you hear that? I'm dead."

"So is he, dear," Lane said, pointing to Edward. "He's dead too."

Vivian's brows rose in astonishment but then she simply looked relieved, throwing her arms around him again. "Thank goodness, I'm not alone. You're really dead?"

"For decades," Edward said proudly, a cocky grin on his face. "And you don't have to cross over if you don't want to. I'm never going to. I know which way I would be going and they aren't going to get me. You can have a fulfilling afterlife, Viv. You can have fun and be with friends. You don't have to cross over. You can be a ghost like me."

Missy groaned and buried her face in her hands. Lane didn't look much happier. Daisy and my mother looked like they didn't know what to say.

Frankly, neither did I.

"Are you sure?" Vivian asked. "I don't have to cross over? I'm a little scared, Eddie. What would I do in the in-between?"

"Anything you want," he answered promptly. "We can do just about anything a living person can. I mean, not everything, of course. I live in the bookstore. I spend my days reading and visiting friends. I'm working on a documentary too. You can keep writing if you want to. In fact, you can come live with me in the bookstore. Then we'll always have company."

Missy's eyes went wide with panic. I thought my friend's head was going to pop off of her shoulders and spin around a few times. The thought of having Vivian in her bookstore day in and day out for centuries was simply a bridge too far. Even for my sweet, patient friend.

"Now wait one minute," Missy protested. "You cannot just invite anyone you like to live in my bookstore. That's not how this works. It's my bookstore."

"It's my home," Edward protested. "Don't I get a say?"

"No," Missy said with a shake of her head. "It's my bookstore. I let you stay there."

"You couldn't keep me out," he said with a smirk.

"I could," Missy shot back. "Grandma Lane could cast a spell that would make the bookstore impenetrable to spirits."

"Are you–are you threatening me?" Edward asked, looking far more unsure than he had only a moment ago. "Would you really do that to me?"

Missy glanced at Vivian before turning back to Edward. "It's fine for you, but I don't want any more ghosts in the bookstore. At least not right now."

"She's my friend, Missy. I want her there."

"I'm sorry, Edward. I just can't do that."

Biting his lip, Edward turned to Daisy. "Will you take us in? We can live with Charles and Amelia. We wouldn't take up any more space."

"Edward," Missy scolded. "It isn't right to put someone on the spot like that. Daisy already has two ghosts living with her. Maybe she doesn't want four."

I should have known what was going to happen next but I'd been too engrossed in the drama playing out. I'm an idiot.

Edward's attention turned to me. Me? Fantastic. And I say that in a sarcastic way.

"What about you, Tedi? We can stay in your closet with Terrence."

It was bad enough that I had to get dressed in the bathroom

these days. But did I really want cocky and annoying Edward along with arrogant and picky Vivian every day of my short existence?

Um, no. That was an easy question.

Missy threw up her hands. "You're doing it again. You're putting my best friend on the spot. She's too nice to tell you no. You're just being difficult now."

Edward stuck out his chin. "You can't tell me what to do, and Tedi can make her own decisions."

Everyone was waiting for my decision. They were all quiet and looking at me. Oh dear.

"Well...I mean...it's just that...I not only have Terrence, you see. I have an inn full of spirits, although I don't know them by name. Basically...what I'm saying is...I think the inn is full. As in no vacancies."

I felt about two inches tall but I couldn't take them in. There were more spirits in the inn but I didn't interact with them. It didn't mean that they weren't there, though. If I thought that Edward and Vivian would move in and then I'd never hear from them...I might have said yes. But, let's face it, that wasn't going to happen. They were going to be loud and around all the time. My home was a sanctuary from people like...Vivian.

"Vivian can go home with me," Lane announced loudly. "Please note that this is a temporary solution only while she decides what she wants to do. I do expect her to be respectful in my home."

The last was said as a clear warning and Vivian seemed to

have heard. She sniffed that she would, of course, be respectful.

"You, however, young man," Lane went on. "Are not invited. I'm not fond of your attitude, to be honest."

Not many people were.

"I have a place to live," Edward said, his lip curled derisively. "I don't need you."

With his bad attitude, something must have snapped inside of Missy. Normally she was the sweetest, kindest person you'd ever want to meet. But she'd been through a great deal in the last twenty-four hours. A bride can only take so much and with a dead body at her reception she'd reached her limit. She hadn't even wanted to invite Edward but she didn't want to hurt his feelings. Now he was urging the newly passed on not to cross over and inviting them to live in her bookstore.

She couldn't take it anymore.

Missy got up into Edward's face, her finger wagging under his ghostly nose. "You do not have a place to live. I'm done with your acting like no one else matters or has feelings. You're done at the bookstore. You're fired and I don't want you back there. You need to vacate immediately."

I almost staggered back in shock. Missy had been angry before but I'd never seen her like this. She was *furious*.

Edward wasn't any happier. I could feel the anger radiating off of him like a space heater in the corner of a room.

"Fine with me," he spat out. "I don't need your moldy books anyway. I was just staying there because I felt sorry for you. You lead the most boring life of anyone I've ever seen. *And I'm dead.*

So think about that. You'll miss me when I'm gone. I have lots of friends I can stay with. I don't need some pathetic bookstore owner. Good riddance."

With a pop and a rush of cool air he was gone, leaving the rest of us standing in a circle. It had been a strange and crazy day, and I had the sneaking suspicion that it wasn't over yet.

But at least I didn't have two extra ghosts going home with me.

Chapter Five

AFTER EXITING THE ladies' room, I had one heck of a headache. Poor Missy was upset, second-guessing her actions and wondering if perhaps she'd been a bit rash by kicking Edward out. I'd never been Edward's biggest fan, I'll openly admit that. But I think she did the right thing. He had to have known how she would react to him urging Vivian not to cross over. Then to add insult to injury, he'd invited her to live in the bookstore. He'd gone way out of bounds with that.

He and Missy were able to co-exist because they'd come to a mutual understanding, respecting each other's space and privacy. Throwing Vivian into the mix would have been chaos.

Lane and Daisy had ducked out of the reception with Vivian in tow, but stopped to tell me to apologize to Jack for leaving without checking with him first. They would be available to talk to him at his convenience.

"And he can talk to Vivian too. If he wants," Lane had said.

Missy and Dylan had decided to simply have the cake cut and served since everyone was hanging around waiting to give their statements. Sadly, that cake was like sawdust in my mouth after everything that had happened. I'd wanted today to be perfect and it had ended up a disaster.

But somehow, I'd lost my mother in the crowd. I couldn't see her anywhere and I really wanted to talk to her about what we could do for Missy and Dylan. Was there anything we could do? I wasn't even sure.

I thought she might have snuck onto the back patio to make a phone call so I headed in that direction, stepping outside and breathing in the fresh air. Instead of my mother I found Andrea sitting at a small wrought iron table, crying into a shredded tissue. I hadn't exactly been her biggest cheerleader but I couldn't walk away from someone clearly in distress.

"Hey, are you...okay?"

Andrea looked up at me, her face tearstained. Her mascara was running down her cheeks. Even the feathers around her neckline looked droopy.

"It's ruined. It's just ruined. I'll never work in the wedding industry again. My reputation will be in tatters. No one will want a wedding planner that had a murder at the reception. I'll be a pariah in the whole state."

Now I could think of one older woman who was currently lying in my coatroom that was having a much worse day, but Andrea had a point. If this got out, she would definitely have more trouble finding clients.

"I'm sure it won't be so bad. You've got many satisfied and happy clients that will gladly give you excellent references. I'm sure Missy and Dylan will as well. It's not your fault that Vivian is dead."

That made Andrea sob all the harder. I wasn't doing so well at the *cheering up* stuff.

"You'll get a good reference from them, and...you can use me as a reference too. If you want to."

Sniffling, Andrea's eyes brightened. "Really? You'd do that? Because a reference from the owner of a popular inn would really help me. I'd be happy to work more weddings here. I really enjoyed it until...well...you know."

The murder.

"Yes," I found myself saying. I was a sucker for tears. Mine. A friend's. Anyone really. "I will certainly give you a good reference. You did a wonderful job today. None of this is your fault."

Even though the only thing everyone was going to remember was the grisly sight of the dead body. They weren't going to be talking about the great canapés or the rocking band.

"None of this is your fault," I repeated. "A few people might not see that but that's on them. I doubt they're the kind of people you want for a client."

She dabbed at her eyes with her sodden tissue. "You're such a nice person, Tedi. And you're right. Those aren't the kind of people that I want to work for."

I didn't contradict Andrea about whether I was a nice person or not. I'd never really thought of myself as a super nice person. Missy was much nicer than I was. Generally, I was a decent person but I could also be difficult and stubborn. But I wasn't cruel enough to blame the poor wedding planner for a murder. That would be heartless.

"Maybe we should go back inside?" I suggested. "Have you talked to Jack yet? He's going to want your statement."

I didn't know if Jack had some extrasensory perception but right on cue the back door swung open and he strode through it. He was still wearing that grim expression and I kind of wanted to give him some apple pie a la mode to make him feel better.

"Ms. Smith? Do you have a few moments to make a statement? I have a couple questions for you."

Andrea gave a brave smile and swiped at a damp cheek with the back of her hand.

"Of course, Sheriff. Whatever you need."

"What did you see in the minutes leading up to the bouquet toss? Was Vivian at her table? Was anyone else missing?"

Nervously chewing on her bottom lip, Andrea shook her head. "I didn't see anything. I was back in the kitchen making a phone call. My boyfriend has been feeling under the weather. Then I came back out to the main room to announce the flower toss."

"Did you notice anything unusual?"

Andrea shook her head again. "Not really, but my mind was on my reception checklist. Honestly, Sheriff, I'm not sure that I can be that much help to you. There were over two hundred people at the reception and I was running around working all day. I wouldn't notice if someone wasn't seated at their table or if they stepped out to have a cigarette or make a call."

Before Jack could reply, Andrea continued. "But I will tell you that I saw and heard Vivian and Herschel arguing in between the ceremony and the reception. They were standing outside the foyer and they sounded really angry."

"Could you hear what they were saying?" Jack asked, scratching notes on his pad.

"I didn't hear it all, but I heard Vivian say that she was calling her lawyers, and then he said that he'd make her sorry if she did. After that, I figured that it wasn't any of my business and I headed back to the kitchen to check on the canapés."

Jack finished writing in his notebook. "Thank you, Ms. Smith. I appreciate your cooperation. If you think of anything, please let me know. Sometimes it's the smallest things that break a case."

Andrea dabbed at her face with a tissue. "Can I go inside now? I'd like to repair my makeup."

The wedding planner bustled into the building so it was just me and Jack standing outside.

"Are you having any luck?"

"Not really. So far no one is a huge fan of Vivian but everyone says they wouldn't have killed her because of it. Daisy also saw Herschel and Vivian arguing earlier. Dylan swears that Herschel and Bandy are behind this. According to him, they wanted Vivian to invest in some business of theirs and she told them no. They still owe her for the last time she invested in one of the schemes."

"That's probably what Herschel was referring to then," I

said. "Vivian was going to contact her attorney to call in the loans and he was upset about it."

"Maybe," Jack conceded. "I'll need to talk to Vivian, though. Where have you hidden her?"

I should be used to it by now. Jack seemed to know everything about everyone. It was a little spooky but okay because he didn't turn those powers on me.

"You saw us then? I wondered about that."

"I did. Did Grandma Lane cast a spell? Don't worry. No one else saw you except for the other spirits like Terrence, Amanda, and Charles."

"And Edward," I added. "He's upset Missy by convincing Vivian not to go into the light. Then he invited Vivian to live with him at the bookstore."

Jack's brows shot up. "How did Missy take that?"

"Not well. She told Vivian that she couldn't move in and then she told Edward he had to get out right away. She was livid. I don't remember the last time I've seen her that mad. Maybe...when David and I divorced? She was furious with him for being such a jerk."

"So where are Vivian and Edward now?"

"I don't know where Edward is but Vivian is staying temporarily with Grandma Lane. Emphasis on the temporary part. Lane was adamant about that."

Jack rubbed his chin. "Sounds like Missy had a good reason to fly off the handle. Edward's been a bee in everyone's bonnet for a long time now. He's always pushing boundaries. I'm guessing he was like that in life too."

"He says he's never going into the light. He knows which way he's going."

"Pushing boundaries wouldn't send him the wrong way. You have to have a chunk of evil in your soul. As annoying as he is, I'm not sure he qualifies."

"Vivian was concerned about which way she'd go. Do you think she has evil in her soul? Can your demon powers figure that out?"

"I can feel true, unadulterated evil. The watered-down stuff? Not as easily. I trust my gut instinct most of the time. But honestly, the people who are concerned about which way they're going usually are the ones that aren't bad enough to worry about. If they were truly evil, they wouldn't think anything they'd done was that awful."

"It's sounds so simple when you say it like that."

"Humans tend to overcomplicate things."

He said it with a smile but I had a feeling that the statement was directed at me.

"You're saying that I overcomplicate things?"

"A little. Sometimes. You can't help it. It's human nature."

"And you don't have that nature because you aren't human?"

"I'm kind of human, Tedi. No medical doctor would ever know the difference. The doctor that treated my gunshot wound just thinks that I'm an amazing healer. I had to pretend for weeks to be in pain so I didn't freak him out."

"You know, I've never heard that story."

"I'll tell you about it once I clear up this case. Deal?"

It was the best offer I was going to get.

"So what do we do now?"

"We don't do anything. I continue with my investigation and you comfort Missy and Dylan."

Jack was so predictable. He was always telling me to butt out.

"This murder happened in my inn at my best friend's wedding. I think I have a right to be concerned."

"You absolutely do. You can be concerned all you want. But you aren't going to do any investigating. This is my job, and it could be dangerous." He nodded toward the door he'd come through. "We have a killer running around and he or she may not be done yet."

That was a chilling thought.

Chapter Six

MISSY AND DYLAN had gone off alone for a little while and then returned to announce that they were postponing their Mediterranean honeymoon until Vivian's killer was caught. They simply couldn't relax and enjoy themselves knowing that a murderer was loose in Ravenmist.

They'd gathered along with Daisy and my mother in my apartment so they could change into casual clothes. The newly married couple was calmed down by now, resigned that their "special day" had been somewhat of a nightmare.

Dylan was especially worried that his relatives were going to find out about ghosts, demons, the Grim Reaper, and all sort of other fun supernatural goings-on in Ravenmist. I couldn't help him as there was a good chance they'd already interacted with a spirit or two at the wedding.

After changing, they hurried over to Missy's parents' home where Dylan's mom and dad also were. Dylan didn't want his parents to have to deal with Vivian's final arrangements all by themselves as he was certain his Uncle Herschel would be absolutely no help. Alvin, on the other hand, had volunteered to take the lead.

Daisy fell back into the soft cushions of my couch, heaving a heavy sigh. "Heavens to Betsy, it's been a day. I feel like I'm ten years older. Was it only a few hours ago that everything was normal?"

"Normal is not a word I'd use to describe this town most of the time," my mother said. "But I do feel terrible for Missy and Dylan. What a horrible way for the wedding day to end. There's not much we can do to make it better for them either."

I disagreed.

"We can catch the killer as quickly as possible," I argued. "That way they can put this all behind them and go on their honeymoon."

"I'm sure Jack is doing the best he can, Tedi," Daisy said. "But as powerful as he his, he can't just look at someone and know that they're a murderer. It doesn't work like that."

"I wish it did," I said with a sigh. "As long as this is hanging over Missy's and Dylan's heads they're not going to be able to move forward. Personally, I'd want a whole new wedding. This one is tainted."

My mother Peggy grinned and clapped her hands together. "Tedi, you are brilliant."

Well...yeah. But I still needed to ask.

"What did I say that was so brilliant? I'll say it again."

"A new wedding," Peggy said. "We can do that. A nice quiet ceremony just for Dylan and Missy. We need to find just the right place. Somewhere private but lovely. Just a simple ceremony with the people they care about."

"As much as I like the idea, I'm not sure a new wedding is the answer, Mom. They're not going to forget today no matter what we do."

Daisy tapped her chin. "Is there a spell we could do? Something that would make them forget what happened today?"

"Whoa," I said, holding up my hands in a stopping motion. "That's some serious mojo there. You start messing with someone's mind and who knows where you might end up. If we're not careful we could wipe out their memories completely. It sounds dangerous."

I was also getting a little worried that the now "go to" remedy for issues was to *cast a spell*. Heartbroken? Cast a spell. Need the identity of a demon? Cast a spell. Need to make a bride and groom feel better? A spell will do the trick.

Peggy nodded in agreement. "As much as I sort of like the idea, Tedi has a point. We're not real witches and we need to be careful. We don't really know what we're doing and we could do more harm than good."

"You're right," Daisy sighed. "I just want to make everything all better for them."

"You know I'm trying to be more of an optimist," I said, forcing a smile to my face. "Maybe we could look at this as a positive. Like how their marriage has no way to go but up from here."

"Don't challenge the universe, Tedi," my mother warned with a shake of her head. "That's dangerous. Never say things like *it can't get any worse.* Because it can."

"I was just trying to see the bright side."

Peggy reached out and patted my hand. "And I think that's wonderful. Good for you. Knowing Missy and Dylan, that's what they're trying to do now too. But I do think that we can help them. We can't get rid of the bad memories, but we can give them some good ones to help take their place."

I was about to ask if she and Daisy had any ideas when there was a woosh of air and Terrence and Edward were standing in the middle of the living room. Neither of them looked happy. Clearly, they were on the outs. Again.

"You have to ask Tedi," Terrence said, his arms crossed over his chest. "I can't just decide on my own that it's okay."

Edward threw up his hands. "You just don't want me here. Go ahead. Just say it."

"Fine, I don't want you here. This is my home."

Ohhh, I had a terrible feeling about what they were arguing about. It wasn't going to be pleasant.

"I can't believe you said that to me," Edward shouted. "We're supposed to be friends."

"We're friends only when you want us to be. The rest of the time you ignore me. I'm not going to take that anymore."

My heart swelled with pride at Terrence's words. I was so proud of him. Edward was getting a hard lesson that actions had consequences. He'd treated so many people rather shabbily and now his chickens had come home to roost.

To my chagrin, Edward turned his attention to me.

"Terrence says I have to ask you."

If only the ground would open up and swallow me...right...this...second.

No luck.

"Terrence says that I have to ask you if I can live here at the inn."

To be truthful, I was surprised he was asking again. He'd already heard my answer earlier.

"The inn is already full of spirits, Edward. Most of them I don't even know. I think we're full up here."

I could see his expression grow darker. "I don't actually need your permission. I could just stay here."

At some point my mother had stood up. Now she was almost nose to nose with Edward. I wasn't sure he remembered his own mother, but I knew my own. She didn't put up with petulance from her own daughters. She surely wasn't going to with a sixty or seventy-year-old ghost.

"Actually we can," Peggy shot back. "We can cast out any spirit that we don't want living here in the inn. I think you know that."

"You wouldn't do that," Edward replied, his tone more unsure than moments before. "Would you?"

I didn't want him to feel badly but I also didn't want to rock the harmonious boat we had here at the inn.

"Right now we're all balanced," I tried to explain. "Everyone is okay with everyone else and we all live in peace. I don't want to change that by adding in anyone else. I'm very sorry, Edward.

I just don't think the inn is the right home for you."

In a flash, he was gone without replying. I felt like a worm saying no, but I also knew how much trouble he'd caused Missy over the years and I didn't want that here. This was my sanctuary. Edward was fine but in small doses.

"Don't feel guilty, Tedi," Terrence said. He must have been able to read my expression. "Remember that Edward doesn't have to live anywhere. He's a ghost, just like me. We don't get cold or hungry. He can go inhabit any of the buildings in Ravenmist if he wanted to. He wanted to come here because he had something to prove to Missy. He's been getting more and more annoying these last several months. Ever since Missy gave him that job at the bookstore, he's been almost insufferable to be around."

Terrence made a decent point. Edward's behavior – which hadn't been fantastic to begin with – had been going downhill for some time now.

"If you'd brought him into our home," Terrence went on. "Who knows how the other spirits here would have taken that? They might be very upset."

I had always known there were other ghosts in the inn but I'd never actually talked to any of them. Our other residents had existed in quiet anonymity for more years than I even knew. They kept to themselves mostly and I was fine with that.

"I don't want to upset anyone."

"I think you did the right thing, pumpkin," my mother said gently. "Terrence is right. It wouldn't have been fair to everyone else here at the inn. Plus, Edward will be fine. He can choose from literally hundreds of buildings in town to live in. He's not desperate."

"I still feel like a jerk," I sighed. "I like Edward. He's okay. I just…"

"Don't want to live with him," Daisy said, finishing my sentence. "I like Edward too, but like you, I don't want to live with him either. It doesn't make us bad people. We're just not compatible."

Not compatible. I could go with that. It was true. We'd drive each other crazy within twenty-four hours.

And from where I was at the moment? It would be a short trip.

JACK ENDED UP in my kitchen eating apple pie not long after my encounter with Edward. He looked unhappy and tired so I immediately cut him a humongous slab of pie along with a couple of scoops of vanilla ice cream. He didn't say much to me until it was gone so I sat next to him while he ate and gathered his thoughts. I knew he'd tell me what he'd learned in his own time.

"Vivian Dashwood didn't have many friends among the wedding guests," he finally said, tucking the paper napkin under the edge of the plate. "I didn't hear too many nice things about her today, to be honest. Her nephew Alvin seemed genuinely upset that she's dead, but his father and brother are a whole other story."

"Alvin's a nice guy from what I've seen."

Jack chuckled at my omission. "I noticed you didn't say anything about Herschel and Bandy. That was restrained of you."

"I spent a lot of time with my mother today, and she always said that if you can't say anything nice…"

"Don't say anything at all. Good advice. But I am going to ask. What do you think of Herschel and Bandy? I trust your judgment. Most of the time."

"I'm gonna ignore that shot too," I said, rolling my eyes. Just because I wasn't a supernatural being with amazing powers, Jack always had to put a caveat on his statements. "Herschel is always looking for a get rich quick scheme that doesn't require him to do much or any work. Bandy is a lot like his dad, plus he drinks too much and gets handsy."

"Did he get handsy with you?" Jack asked, his expression turning to a frown. "If he–"

"Relax, I can handle him. I've met a heck of a lot worse. He's harmless."

"Maybe. He and his dad might have a motive to kill Vivian."

"Money?"

"It's a powerful motivator."

"Did you ask Herschel what he and Vivian were arguing about before the reception?"

"I did and he says that he has no idea what I'm talking

about. He never talked to her. The conversation didn't happen."

"Andrea clearly said that it did."

"I told him there was a witness, but he swears that he's telling the truth."

I wasn't sure that I would believe Herschel over Andrea. Not that I knew her well – I didn't – but I could see Herschel bending the truth to fit his agenda.

"Andrea doesn't have a motive to lie."

"I agree. I told Herschel that I would need to talk to him again tomorrow. I'll see if he sticks to his story or meanders away from it a bit after getting to sleep on it."

"Will you need my drawing room? Or did you want to do this at the station?"

"I wouldn't mind using your drawing room. It's handy for me, and for you too. You can listen in so I don't have to tell you about it later."

It took my brain a few seconds to process Jack's words.

He knew.

I should have been shocked but I wasn't.

"How long have you known?"

"Since the beginning," he said with a smile. "I could feel you on the other side of the wall."

"Why didn't you say anything?"

I couldn't decide if I was mad, frustrated, or relieved. Maybe all three.

"Because it was important to you. And you weren't hurting anything. But I still think you should leave the law enforcement up to me, Tedi. I don't want you getting hurt."

"I'm really not trying to find murderers. They just seem to find me."

"And that's my biggest worry. Trouble seems to go out of its way to find you."

That was sweet. He was worried about me.

"What else did you learn today?"

"I'll tell you, but I don't suppose I could get a sandwich to go with that pie?"

He could. With his help, I made him a stacked roast beef sandwich with a side of potato chips.

"I talked to Alvin also." Jack munched on his chips. "He said that he didn't see his father or brother after dinner. Apparently, they went outside to make a phone call and he didn't see them come back."

"It seems like everyone uses their phone as an alibi these days."

"They should be aware that I can check phone logs. If they weren't on a call, I'll know about it."

"Maybe they were playing Candy Crush and don't want to admit it."

"I can find that out too."

"Did you talk to Sadie, Vivian's assistant?"

"I did. She says that Vivian was in a good mood all day, mostly because of Edward's presence. At one point after dinner, Vivian excused herself to go to the ladies' room and Sadie didn't see her after that. She did say that she saw Vivian and Bandy talking in the foyer during the toasts. Vivian was laughing and Bandy was angry. She said she couldn't hear the conversation so she doesn't know what they were discussing. I'm going to need to talk to Edward. He was the closest one to Vivian all day."

"That might be a little difficult," I said with a groan. "He pretty much hates me right about now. He asked to stay here and I said no."

"He asked again?"

I recounted the entire discussion between Terrence, Edward, and myself in the living room to Jack, and how my mother had even had a few words for our annoying spirit.

"I can't say that I blame her," Jack finally said when I was done. "Edward can be a piece of work at times."

"I feel like a terrible person not letting him live here."

"Did you want him to live here? How did Terrence feel about it?"

"I didn't and Terrence was against it too. I don't know how the other spirits would feel about it."

Jack's gaze ran over the kitchen. "Just how many do you have in the inn?"

"I have no idea. We have the odd thing out of place or the occasional transparent figure in the corner of your eye, but I don't bother them and they don't bother me. We have a good thing going."

"And Edward would have thrown that into chaos."

"Probably."

"Then you did the right thing."

"Then why do I feel so horrible about it?"

"Because you're a nice person."

"I don't think that I'm all that nice. Missy is nice. Me? Sometimes."

"And Missy kicked Edward out. What does that tell you? And I think you're nice. You just don't take any guff. You're not a doormat. That's a good thing, Tedi."

"I just wish the whole day had gone differently. This was supposed to be some wonderful day and now it's all screwed up. I can't change that either."

"Once I find the killer, Missy and Dylan can move on from this."

"I'll do whatever I can to help."

"No, you won't."

Jack was so stubborn. He always thought he knew best.

"I will."

"No, Tedi. You won't. You'll keep out of this investigation. I don't want to have to worry about you and your safety while I'm trying to do my job."

"Missy is my best—"

"And I'm the sheriff. I know you want to help, but you need to leave this to me. I'll find out who murdered Vivian. I promise."

Jack didn't make many promises, especially about investigations.

"Besides, aren't you doing some other important research?" he asked, his brow quirked in question.

Oh…that. Yes, I was. Today, however, I'd forgotten about apocalyptic warnings and the eternal battle between good and evil. There were evil demons out there that wanted to wipe humanity from the face of the earth. Ravenmist was ground zero for that war. It was probably time to get back to that.

Jack could find a murderer while I would look for the key to stop the world from ending.

We both had a critical job to do.

Chapter Seven

THE NEXT MORNING I'd barely had my first cup of coffee when I was accosted by a frantic Andrea. She looked upset, her usually unflappable exterior long gone. Her hair was slightly askew, and she was wearing sweatpants and a t-shirt instead of her usual garish outfits. She looked so different that I almost didn't recognize her until she was close up.

"Tedi, thank goodness I've found you. I really need to talk to you."

I held up my half full cup.

"I need a refill. Do you want some coffee?"

Oops! I'd forgotten that Andrea didn't imbibe caffeine. Although I had to say that she kind of looked like she could use it today.

"No, thank you. I'm fine. But you go ahead."

"It can wait. What can I help you with?" I gestured toward my office door. "Do you want to go sit down?"

Andrea nodded and I led her into my office. She sat in the guest chair, right next to Howard the Fern and I settled behind my desk.

I could get a full cup of coffee later. Maybe a danish too.

Andrea leaned forward, her palms on the edge of my desk. "Do you know how the investigation is going? Is the sheriff close to arresting anyone?"

There was no telling what Jack had been up to in the last eight hours or so. He needed far less rest than normal humans did, but he did eventually sleep.

"The last I heard he was interviewing guests."

She sat back, her hands wringing together until the knuckles were white.

"The sheriff asked me not to leave town."

That was standard.

"But I have clients and events that I need to take care of. I live in Castville and I really need to get back there. I have a cat that can't stay by herself for long. Can't you talk to him? Explain my situation? He's your boyfriend, right?"

Right. Yes. Jack was my boyfriend. We'd been dating for months now, but I was still getting used to that moniker. He wasn't a boy and we weren't teenagers anymore. It didn't seem a title that really fit two adults but at this point I didn't have a replacement.

Significant other? Sort of cold.

Man friend? That sounded creepy.

Wait…what were we talking about? Ah yes, Andrea wanted to leave town and go back home. I didn't think it would be a big deal. She was only thirty minutes away and she didn't even know Vivian so she didn't have a motive.

"I can ask him but he'd have to have assurance that you'd be available if he needed to talk to you again."

Actually, Jack couldn't stop her from leaving Ravenmist. Not one bit. But I didn't tell her that.

"That would be great, awesome. Thank you so much. I really do need to leave today."

She looked at me expectantly. I realized she wanted me to talk to Jack. Now.

"I'm going to take him some breakfast and I'll talk to him then."

I hadn't planned on that, the idea had just popped into my head, but it sounded like a good one. Normally, he'd just order takeout at Daisy's but I know he'd easily eat a second breakfast. It would be a nice thing to do for my...*boyfriend.*

Nope, I still didn't like the sound of it. I really needed to give this some thought.

Andrea thanked me and left, leaving me with my half-empty coffee cup. I headed into the kitchen for a refill and some food for Jack.

This could also be my chance to find out the latest on the investigation. Just because I wasn't helping didn't mean that I wasn't interested.

I WAS WITH Jack less than ten minutes when he received a call from Grandma Lane that Vivian was ready to talk to him. I thought for sure that he'd tell me to go back to the inn but for some reason he let me tag along. Maybe I was finally wearing him down.

When we arrived at Lane's home, I expected to see Missy and Dylan but to my surprise they weren't there. Lane told me that they were with Dylan's parents this morning but would be around later.

Vivian was sitting in Lane's living room watching a morning talk and news show. Being a new spirit, she didn't look as solid as Edward or Terrence. She didn't have the energy yet. She was so transparent I could see the flowered pattern on the sofa cushions.

"Vivian Dashwood, I'm Sheriff Jack Garrett. I was hoping I could ask you a few questions about yesterday."

"You mean about my death? Of course, you can. I want whoever did this to go to jail for a long time."

Her tone was laced with bitterness but I could hardly blame her. She'd been murdered less than twenty-four hours ago.

Jack sat across from her and I perched on the rocking chair in the corner. Lane sat next to Vivian and patted her on the hand in a comforting manner.

"It's okay, Viv. Just answer Jack's questions. He'll find out who did this to you."

Vivian gave Lane a grateful look. One I'd never expected to see on the woman.

"What would you like to know, Sheriff?"

"Did you see who hit you?"

Vivian shook her head. "No, I was all alone in the room. I was on the phone with my interior decorator for the house in Martha's Vineyard telling her that I didn't want any green in the house. I hate green. Anyway, I heard footsteps and I was about to end the call and turn around. And that's it. That's all I remember. Next thing I knew I was in the ladies' room and was being told that I was dead. I don't have any memories of anything in between those two events. Now I'm dead. Not that anyone cares. I don't even know which way I'll go if I cross over into the light."

"Your family and friends have crossed over," Lane said. "You might get to see them again. Wouldn't that be nice?"

"I'd like to see my mother and Henry again. But what if I go the other way?"

"There's no way of knowing. I'm sure you've done good things in your life."

Vivian's lips pressed together in a thin line. "I did everything I could for my family. I worked two jobs until my books started to sell. I worked my fingers to the bone. Then I realized that they were ungrateful wretches. They only wanted what I could give them. They weren't interested in working for anything themselves. Everyone except Alvin and Dylan. Those boys were always sweet to me. They never asked me for anything. I spoiled the others too much."

"You and Herschel argued yesterday," Jack said. "Right before the reception. You were also seen arguing with Bandy later on. What was it about?"

Vivian sighed. "The usual. Money. Herschel and Bandy wanted me to invest in another of their business ventures. I have in the past but every single one has gone belly up. Herschel, and Bandy for that matter, don't like to work. So I told them no. They got angry."

"Did they threaten you?" Jack asked.

"They said I'd be sorry but I wasn't worried. I knew they wouldn't do anything to me."

"You don't think Herschel is capable of murder?"

"Frankly, I think he's too lazy. That goes double for Bandy. But that's not the reason that Herschel wouldn't kill me."

"What is the reason?"

"He and I have a history, you see." She seemed at a loss for words for a moment. "How do I say this delicately? I guess there's no other way than to just say it. Herschel is in love with me."

Love? That's not what love looked like to me. Was Vivian confused?

Jack scratched a few more notes in his pad of paper. "Herschel was in love with you? How do you know this?"

"He told me so."

That had Jack's attention. Heck, it had all of our attention.

"He told you? Recently?"

"No, it's been almost fifty years."

That was a long time.

"Fifty years?" Jack repeated. "Herschel told you fifty years ago that he loved you? Is that right? Are you sure?"

"Very sure." Vivian did sound confident. "We were planning to be married, after all."

Hold the phone…married? Lane and I exchanged an amazed look.

"You and Herschel were going to be married?" I asked, butting in on Jack's questioning. I couldn't help myself. "Fifty years ago? Then what happened?"

Vivian smiled as if remembering something lovely and wonderful.

"At the last minute, I ran off with Herschel's brother Henry. We were married in a small ceremony in Las Vegas. I miss my Henry. He was a wonderful man. So loving. So generous."

Vivian had run off with Herschel's brother and married him instead? And she didn't think Herschel might not be a little…miffed about that? Might want revenge?

I had questions. So many questions.

As far as I was concerned, Herschel had more than one good reason to want Vivian Dashwood dead.

BACK AT THE inn with Jack, I was still reeling from Vivian revealing that she and Herschel had once been engaged.

To be married.

To each other.

Then she'd run off with his brother Henry a few weeks before the wedding. She didn't think Herschel might be honked off about that at all. When I asked her if Herschel was mad or hurt, she'd just said that he was mostly relieved. She didn't think that he truly wanted to get married. They'd been having issues for some time.

Apparently, he'd got over his feelings pretty fast and had ended up marrying some other woman a few years later, bringing two sons – Bandy and Alvin – into the world. Vivian and Henry had never wanted children so they'd been the adoring aunt and uncle, spoiling their nephews.

Eventually, Henry had passed away and Herschel's fortunes had taken a turn. He'd asked Vivian for money and she'd given it. And then again. And again. You get the idea. Recently, she'd decided that he'd had enough help and she'd cut him off.

But she still didn't think he'd kill her over it.

Now that, folks, is optimism.

After talking to Vivian, Jack and I had returned to the inn so he could once again talk to Herschel, armed with a bit more information than he'd had yesterday. He also wanted to speak with Sadie again regarding Vivian's financial picture.

Jack met with Herschel in my drawing room. Yes, I was sitting on the other side of the wall listening in. He knew about it so I didn't feel guilty this time.

Okay, just a *pinch* guilty since Herschel didn't know, but I told myself that he might be a cold-blooded killer and that made me feel better. I'd settled on top of a stack of shoeboxes when Jack started his questioning.

"So you and Vivian were engaged at one point?"

There was an audible snort before Herschel answered.

"Yes, about two hundred years ago. I can barely remember it. We were young and she was beautiful. Thank the heavens that I didn't actually marry her. It would have been a nightmare."

"She jilted you."

"She did me a favor. She made my poor brother's life a misery until the day he died."

"A misery? How?"

"Henry wanted children. He always had. But Vivian didn't. But she didn't tell him that until after they were married. Or how he wanted to live a quiet, small town life. Oh no, they couldn't do that. Vivian had to be seen traveling in the best social circles. She had to go to parties and nightclubs. She dragged my brother around New York City for over twenty years. He hated every minute of it."

"But he didn't leave her. He could have at any time."

"Let's just say she had him on a short financial leash."

"So she made the money?"

"And used it as a weapon on him every single day. Henry had dreams of his own. Big dreams. But she never let him do anything that wasn't in service to her precious writing career. It was the most important thing in her life. The money. The fame. My poor brother always came in second place."

"So what happened after he passed away? It sounds like you borrowed money from Vivian several times."

"I didn't borrow any money. She invested in a few business ventures."

"How did those 'business ventures' do?"

There was a small silence before Herschel responded.

"They didn't do well. Not every investment is going to make money. I told Vivian that there were no guarantees. She understood that. She'd been writing books for fifty years, Sheriff. She's wealthy. I doubt she even noticed the losses."

"So what were you and Vivian arguing about yesterday? And don't say that you weren't. There are witnesses."

There was a noisy sigh from Herschel.

"She and I were discussing the possibility of investing in my new business venture. It's a nightclub in New York City. I thought it would be right up her alley since she loves to socialize."

"And did she say yes or no?"

Jack already knew that answer. I wondered whether Herschel would tell the truth.

"She said that she wasn't interested."

"And that upset you?"

"I thought she was being short-sighted. A trendy club in the city is a license to print money."

"Apparently she didn't agree."

"As I said…short-sighted. I have other potential investors. If Vivian didn't want to be in that was fine."

"Other investors? Such as?"

"For example, I talked to Dylan's best man Zack Thomas. He might be interested."

I had a feeling that was a lie. Zack had been laughing at

Herschel, not shaking hands for a business deal.

"So you're saying that you had no reason to kill her?"

"Not a one."

"Even though you hated the way she treated your brother?"

"I did but not enough to kill someone, Sheriff. That would be crazy. It certainly wouldn't bring Henry back or let him relive the last twenty years of his life. It wouldn't change the past. I may not have liked Vivian all that much, but I didn't kill her."

He sounded very definite and Jack didn't push him, thanking Herschel for answering his questions. I heard the door open and then close, a few footsteps.

"Thanks for talking to me again, Sadie. I do appreciate it."

"It's fine, Sheriff. How can I help you?"

Jack cleared this throat. "You've said that you worked for Vivian Dashwood for the last three years. So would you say that you were close?"

"As in friends? No, I wouldn't say that. Vivian didn't confide in me, if that's what you're asking. I did know a great deal about her life, though, because I organized most of it. I kept her calendar, managed the house staff, made sure she took her medicine. Those sorts of things."

"Medicines? Vivian was talking prescription meds?"

"She was seventy years old, Sheriff. While she was in great shape, she still had a few issues. High cholesterol being one of them. Not because of her diet. As I said, Vivian was quite healthy, but she said it was hereditary. Occasionally, she'd also get migraines. She had a prescription for that also."

"I would imagine working at a computer all day might trigger those. Would you describe Vivian as a workaholic?"

"No. I wouldn't." There was an awkward silence before Sadie continued. "Listen, when I first started working for Vivian she wrote every day from nine in the morning until noon. Rain or shine. Weekend or weekday. It didn't matter. She was a machine when it came to production. It was impressive. But all of that changed."

My interest was piqued. C'mon, Sadie. Spill it.

"Vivian hasn't written anything in about a year. Not a word. It took her months to write her last one and even then, I didn't think she was going to make her deadline. She kept procrastinating and then finally wrote it, but she had to work some awful hours to do it. Since then she's barely gone into her office. She's supposed to have another book done in about a month but as far as I know she hasn't written a word of it. Of course, now that she's gone she won't have to worry about it."

"Did anything happen in Vivian's life that coincided with that? A personal setback? Anything professional?"

"Not that I know of. After she finished the last book, she started actively avoiding her office. It was weird. She had a million excuses why she wasn't going to write on any given day."

"So you would say that she'd been acting strangely for the last year?"

"Yes, I would say that."

"But you don't know why?"

"I don't. It's a complete mystery to me."

Interesting. It sounded like Jack needed to have another talk with Vivian. What had changed in her life that she would just...stop writing? For someone who had been so prolific over the years, it didn't make sense.

The questioning was over and I carefully slipped out of my closet only to run into Terrence, who was leaning over his laptop. He loved social media.

"How are you doing, Terrence? Big plans today?"

He looked up from the screen and shook his head. "I might go over and hang out with Charles and Amelia later."

I hated to ask but...

"Have you heard from Edward?"

He grimaced, his nose wrinkling slightly. "No, and I don't expect to. You know how he is. He's gone off to sulk for awhile. Eventually he'll come back, admit he was wrong and then apologize. But until then he's going to be scarce."

"I hope he's okay."

"He's fine. Nothing bad can happen to him."

"Losing all of his friends would be pretty awful."

"He hasn't lost me. Or you, I bet. If he apologizes, I'll forgive. You'll forgive him. Missy will too. He's just being stubborn because he doesn't like to be wrong."

I grabbed a soda from the fridge. "Do you know his story? All I know is that he says he knows which way he's going."

"I don't, but it's bad. He said that if anyone knew they would never be friends with him."

That didn't sound good.

"I'm going to go see Daisy. Do you want to come with me?"

He was heads down again over the laptop. "Maybe later. Have fun."

So much had happened. So many suspects, but little information to go on.

I needed a slice of apple pie to work this one out.

Chapter Eight

L ATER THAT NIGHT I was sitting in my apartment watching a cooking show and eating some microwave popcorn when I heard a knock on my door. Despite basically living where I work, it wasn't a common occurrence. My staff would text me if they needed me and Missy or my mother would just barge in. That meant it could only be one person – Jack.

I opened the door and ushered him in, offering him a beer from my refrigerator and my bowl of popcorn. He sat down next to me on the couch and didn't say anything for awhile, just munching away at the salty, buttery goodness before us and sipping at his beer. It was only when the show finished that he finally spoke.

"I told Andrea that she could leave town. I'm guessing she'll check out sometime tomorrow. She's a permanent resident of this area and a business owner, so if I have any questions I should be able to find her."

"When she asked me I didn't know what to tell her."

He shrugged and placed the almost empty bowl on the coffee table. All that was left were the hard kernels and I didn't like those much. "It's fine. I can't really stop her and I'm guessing she knows that. I thought it was nice that she even asked."

I wasn't as sure as Jack was that Andrea knew but it didn't matter if he was okay with it.

"I hate to ask the obvious question, but how is the case going?"

"About like you would expect. Pretty much everyone disliked Vivian so they had a motive."

"Alvin didn't. Neither did Dylan."

"Okay, she had two people who didn't hate her guts. Everyone else? Loathed her."

"She didn't seem all that bad at Lane's house. She was almost…nice."

"What I've learned about her would curl your hair, Tedi. She's not nice."

I pulled at a red curl and watched it spring back. "Uh, I've already got those curls covered."

Chuckling, Jack shifted on the couch, stretching his long legs. "Then it would straighten your hair. Vivian Dashwood had a mean streak a mile wide. I received the background on her from my buddy in Chicago and it was eye-opening. She was mean to other authors, crappy to business partners, and worse to her own family. The only people she treated halfway decently were her readers and that was because she kept them at arms' length. I assume so they wouldn't see what she was really like. Trust me when I say that there are no shortage of people that are happy to see her dead. The suspect list is a mile long."

"Can't it be cut down to who was at the wedding?"

"Theoretically, yes. Although someone who wasn't invited could have snuck into the reception. I noticed that you haven't put any security cameras around the convention center yet."

"So this is my fault?"

I'd been meaning to do it but with the wedding and everything...

"Not at all. It would just make things easier if I could confirm that no one else was there. I could also confirm some of the alibis. I swear half the people at the reception were on their cell phones at the time of the murder. What does that even say about our society as a whole?"

Jack didn't like cell phones much. I wasn't a big fan either. We had that in common. They had their place but I wasn't glued to it for hours and hours a day. I was a tad suspicious of technology. It was supposed to save me time, but where did all the saved time go anyway? I sure wasn't benefitting from it. Was it being sucked into some cosmic black hole?

"Nothing good, I would wager. So which way are you leaning? Herschel and Bandy? They seem like they have more than enough motive. Or what about Sadie? I bet Vivian was an awful employer."

"You're leaving out Alvin. Or Dylan. Or Dylan's parents. Or anyone that actually knew Vivian."

"Alvin loved his great-aunt."

"He says he does. The question would be *why*? She doesn't seem to treat him any better than anyone else. While Dylan doesn't hate Vivian, he doesn't seem to love her either. He actively stays away from her which I can understand."

"Dylan would never commit murder. Get real. Are we going to do this again? Missy and Dylan are not killers."

"I agree Missy is not a killer. With that huge white ball gown she was difficult to miss, so I have a minute by minute run down of everywhere she was the entire reception. Dylan, on the other hand, was in a dark suit along with dozens of other men. He could get lost in a crowd. I haven't been able to get a fix on his whereabouts at the time of the murder. He's still a suspect until I can clear him. And before you get all upset, I'm actively trying to clear him. I don't want Dylan to be a killer, Tedi. Give me a little credit."

"Dylan isn't a killer."

"I agree, but I still have to prove it."

"So what do you think about Herschel and Bandy?" I asked again. "Do you think they did it?"

"They certainly had a strong motive. I'm looking into their backgrounds to see what I can find out."

"So you're leaning that direction?"

Sighing, he shook his head. "I'm leaning in several directions. Sadie isn't out of the realm of possibility either."

"Are you checking into her background too?"

"I am. But to be honest I think this case is going to come down to forensics. Hair, fibers, fingerprints."

"You have fingerprints?"

This was news. He'd never said a word.

"We have fingerprints."

"On the murder weapon?"

"Yes. Unfortunately, several sets. Yours are probably there too, so don't get too excited."

Until the murder I would have assumed that I was the last person to touch the bookends. Or maybe one of my employees could have moved them. Then their fingerprints would be there as well.

Jack finished his beer and stood to toss it into my kitchen garbage. I had to admit that he was an extremely tidy man. David had just dropped things all over the house and he swore that his eyesight was bad so he couldn't see dust or lint. I'd caught Jack about a month ago scrubbing my kitchen sink because he'd poured some out-of-date milk down the drain. It only served to make him even more attractive.

"Should I ask about our other pressing matters?" I asked.

"You mean the eradication of all mankind from the earth? What would you like to know?"

"You said that you were looking for powerful supernatural objects that might be able to help us. Any progress?"

"I said that there *might* be supernatural objects that could help us." He tapped on a kitchen cabinet. "I don't suppose you have any snacks in here? I'm starving."

As a demon, Jack needed about a trillion calories a day. Now that I knew the truth about him, I had his back. I kept a huge stash of food in my refrigerator and kitchen when before I would have been lucky to have bread and peanut butter.

"There's snack food in the cabinet and a leftover pot roast in the refrigerator from the dining room."

In other words, I didn't make it. I was a decent cook but my chef was a whole other level of amazing.

I could see Jack wavering. He wanted the pot roast and probably the snacks too, but he didn't want to be a bad guest.

"Go ahead," I waved at him. "I brought them here for you, knowing you'd be hungry. There's a banana cream pie for dessert. Help yourself."

Better he eat than me. A slice of pie was one thing, but a whole one wasn't anything I needed. Unless I wanted to buy an entirely new wardrobe.

With a grimace, Jack relented rummaging in my refrigerator and making himself a plate. "You're spoiling me, Tedi. You don't have to do this. I won't starve."

"I'm not so sure about that. Besides, it was just going to go to waste, and you know how I hate that. Now tell me about your research and I'll tell you about mine."

"You first," he said, tucking into a pot roast sandwich. "I'll eat, you talk."

"You better eat quick because I don't have much to say. Daisy, Missy, Mom, and even Grandma Lane have been combing through old books of magic. We've found nothing. Nada. So now it's your turn."

"I've been talking to some of my friends, seeing what they know. So far I haven't found anything."

"And by friends you mean other demons?"

"Yes."

Just checking.

"Will I ever meet these other demons?"

"At some point, I would say yes. Some are truly my friends and some are more…like work colleagues." Then he grinned, patting a paper napkin at the corners of his mouth. "You may already have met several demons in your lifetime, Tedi. We don't wear name tags."

"What if Orien comes back and we don't have any objects to help?"

"Then I'll fight him myself. I am pretty powerful on my own. I have the power from both of my parents. The only thing I don't have is their gifts."

"Can you explain the whole gifts thing to me again? I don't think I'm clear on it."

He'd mentioned this a few times in passing but hadn't really explained it.

"All demons have gifts, but they can be completely different from one to another. It's left up to fate as to what you get. Some gifts can be inherited, but most cannot. For example, my mother could read minds but I can't."

"Thank goodness. That would have been awkward."

Having Jack being able to read my mind sounded like a nightmare. I'd be incredibly embarrassed. No one needed to know how often I thought about chocolate. That was for me and me alone.

"Would have come in handy as a cop though," he said, leaning against the kitchen counter. "It would make my job so much easier. I'd be able to solve all these murders that keep happening."

The way he said that last statement had my attention. There was something in his tone that told me he was bothered by it.

"I know you don't like murder."

"No one likes murder." He exhaled noisily, his shoulders tight with frustration. "I can't help but wonder…"

"Yes…?"

"Is it me?" he finally said after a moment's silence. "Am I the reason that all of these murders are happening? Did I bring some sort of bad energy into Ravenmist?"

If that were the case, Jack would never forgive himself. He was all about protecting this town, not hurting it.

"I highly doubt it. You have brought a bunch of energy to Ravenmist but I think we can say that it hasn't been malevolent. No one has been hurt by it. The ghosts are happy and everyone seems healthy. I doubt your energy is just going around town and randomly killing people that visit here. That doesn't make any sense. Did the murder rate go up in Chicago when you lived there?"

"Actually, it went down."

"Well, there you go. It's not you."

"Then what is it? And if it's not just chance, how do I stop it?"

That was the million-dollar question. All we needed now was an answer.

I WAS BLISSFULLY drinking my first cup of coffee of the day the next morning in my office. As a business owner, there always seemed to be a million calls to make and a never-ending stack of paperwork to deal with. I'd ignored all but the most urgent last week during the run up to the wedding but I couldn't ignore it any longer. I needed to buckle down and get some work done.

I'd already spoken to Missy and she and Dylan were spending the day with her family. She'd asked me if Jack had made any progress. I almost cried when she did because there was so much hope in her tone. Certainly, she and Dylan wanted to put all of this behind them and go on their honeymoon. I told her that Jack thought the forensics were a good bet to solve the crime. I did not mention that it could take days or weeks to get the results of the lab's tests.

So I was head down over a spreadsheet when I heard a soft knock, but not on my door. A chill ran over me and then Terrence was standing in the middle of my office. I was thrilled that he was learning to knock before entering a room.

"Tedi, do you have a minute?"

"For you? I have five or ten. What's on your mind? Is there an issue with your work?"

Terrence did my weekly supply inventory and it has never been so organized. I'd fought hiring him for months too. He did such a good job I should probably give him a raise. Hey, do you think a ghost from the 1920s could learn to do spreadsheets?

To my surprise, he turned and closed my office door.

"No issue with work. It's all fine." He shifted on his feet awkwardly. "Tedi, I have a confession to make."

Uh oh, this didn't sound good.

"You know you can tell me anything, right? I won't be mad."

I couldn't even imagine being angry at Terrence.

"I heard you and Jack talking last night," he said, the words coming out in a rush.

"Okay."

I wasn't sure what the problem was.

Terrence shoved his hands in the pockets of his trousers, his gaze on the floor.

"Normally when Jack comes over, I leave the apartment so you two can be alone. But I didn't last night. I didn't want to go anywhere so I stayed. I also chose not to let you know that I was there." He looked up, his expression pained. "I wanted to hear if you and Jack were talking about getting married, like Missy and Dylan. If you and Jack get married, you'll move in with him and Tyler and I'll be all alone."

Whoa, this was a lot to take in. Terrence and I had talked about this sort of thing a long time ago but clearly, we were due for a new one.

"First of all, the apartment is your home, Terrence. I don't ever want you to feel like you have to leave it because I have a guest over. Even if it's Jack. Both he and I assume that you're there even if we cannot see you. It's your home. Heck, you were there before me. I'm not upset at all that you stayed last night."

Terrence seemed to visibly relax, almost smiling now.

"As for Jack and I getting married…oh heavens, that's a can of worms right there. I can say with great surety that neither one of us is looking to get married."

Terrence frowned. "Ever? That doesn't seem very realistic."

Okay, *Ever* was a really long time.

"Let's just say that we aren't looking to get married anytime in the near future. If he and I do start talking about it, you'll be one of the first people to know. And trust me when I say this, I will never live in that beige cracker box of a condo he calls a home. No way. If anything I'd build an addition onto the inn or build another house on the property. Wherever I go, you're welcome. End of story. You're…family."

Look at me, folks. Being all optimistic about marriage some-day way off in the future. I feel like I've grown as a human being.

But I'm still not looking to tie the knot.

And Terrence was family. He was the brother that I'd never had but always wanted.

"I think of you as family too, Tedi." He seemed to hesitate for a moment before continuing on. "Your grandma was family as well. And after hearing your conversation with the sheriff last night I think I need to tell you something that she talked to me about many years ago. I remember her discussing objects with powers. Huge powers, and she was afraid of them."

I immediately perked up at his words. Objects? With powers?

"Grandma talked to you about objects with powers? What

kind of objects? What powers?"

He shrugged. "She never said specifically. She said that she was afraid of them, though, so she hid them in the tunnel so that no one could find them. She didn't want them to fall into the wrong hands."

Hmmm…it made me wonder just how much my grandmother had known about the battle between good and evil. Could she have had a demon in her own life? Stranger things had happened in Ravenmist, and I'd even witnessed some of it.

"She hid them in the tunnel?"

"I'm pretty sure that's what she said, but it has been a long time. She said they had some sort of energy. Your grandma was sensitive like that, but she didn't know what they did or how to use them. She said it would be best to make sure they were protected so she hid them."

This was some of the best news I'd heard in a long time. I had to find those objects. I could probably use some help though. Time to talk to Daisy and my mom.

"Terrence, thank you. You're amazing."

This just might be the break we'd been hoping for.

I CALLED MY mom and Daisy right away and we all met at the Grateful Raven, of course. By the time I got there my mom and Daisy were already working on slices of apple pie. I ordered a slice of coconut meringue and a coffee.

"We need to go down to the tunnel and search," Peggy said as I took my first bite of delicious pie. It tasted like a little bit of fluffy heaven. "We should do it as soon as possible."

I didn't disagree, except...

"It could be dangerous," I said. "We don't know what these objects do or how to use them. Grandma hid them because she was afraid of their power. I think that we need to think about that. We could end up destroying ourselves or the town if we aren't careful."

Peggy tapped her chin. "Your grandmother was a smart woman, and I always respected her. She never mentioned any of this to me or your father from what I know. She never mentioned Terrence or supernatural objects. She did say that she believed in ghosts but pretty much everyone in town does, so I didn't think it was anything out of the ordinary."

"Maybe she thought people wouldn't believe her if she said she had a ghost in her closet," Daisy suggested. "It's one thing to say that you believe, but it's a whole other thing to say that you have a ghost as a friend and chat with them every day. That's a different level."

"It is," Peggy conceded. "I just wish she had told us. We could have been years ahead of this...whatever is happening. I feel like we're always one step behind. Getting one of these sacred objects could finally give us the advantage we've been looking for."

"We don't even know what we're looking for," I reminded her. "The term *object* is pretty gosh darn vague. It could be a rock or a necklace or a fork. We just don't know. Even Jack doesn't know all of the objects and what they do, and he was born a demon."

Daisy was drumming her fingers on the table. "We could cast some sort of finding spell. Or maybe a spell to protect us when we're looking."

Here we go again. Did I need to speak up? No one else seemed to be doing it.

"About that…I'm a little worried that our go-to plan is somehow always coming up with some kind of spell. We're not witches. We have no idea what we're doing. If we're not careful we'll turn ourselves into toads."

And while I looked fabulous in green, I didn't want to spend my life as a toad, eating flies. Ick.

Daisy's cheeks turned pink. "You're right. I may get carried away about that. The few spells we've done have gone okay, but it's possible that we simply may have been lucky."

"I'm going to talk to Jack," I said. "He has powers that I still don't understand but I'm sure he can protect us if we go look for the objects. I know he'll want to go with us either way."

Peggy nodded and smiled. "Sometimes I forget that we have him on our side. Of course he should be with us when we search. We'll be safe as kittens with Jack."

My phone buzzed and I checked my messages. A text from my front desk manager to return to the inn right away. There was a problem.

Vivian Dashwood's attorney just showed up to read the will. Come back as fast as possible.

Now this was a turn I didn't expect.

Chapter Nine

I JOGGED BACK to the inn – yes, I can jog if it's important enough – only to find my lobby in an uproar when I arrived. It was filled with Missy, Dylan, and his family, along with Sadie, Andrea, and a man I didn't recognize but from his stuffy blue suit and briefcase I guessed he was the attorney. Everyone was talking loudly over one another and frankly, the entire scene made me want to turn right around and run the other way. I didn't, however, as the minute Missy saw me she ran over and wrapped her arms around me.

"This is awful," she whispered. "We had no idea this was going to happen."

"It will be fine," I said in my best calm voice. "He'll read the will and it will all be fine."

I'd said *fine* twice in a short span of time. I had a terrible feeling it wasn't going to be *fine*.

Missy nodded toward the doors of the drawing room. "We have another problem."

I wasn't following, although the look on her face told me that she thought I should know what she was talking about.

"You're going to have to give me a hint. I got nothing here."

She pressed her fingertips to her temples as if she had a terrible headache. Heck, she probably did.

"Vivian is here. In the drawing room."

I had to replay those words in my head several times before they made sense. Why on earth would Vivian want to be here while the will was read? She already knew what was in it.

"Has anyone seen her?"

I decided to go with an innocuous question.

"No, she's invisible right now. Grandma Lane is in the drawing room too. She told Vivian that if she wanted to watch the reading of the will, she couldn't be seen. Just in case Vivian gets other ideas, Grandma has cast a spell over the room. No one will see them at all."

Just like at the reception. That certainly was a handy dandy spell to have.

"How is Grandma Lane doing with Vivian? Are they...getting along?"

"It's so weird but yes. They sit around and play cards and Gran is teaching Vivian how to bake pie. It's sort of disturbing, but it seems to be working. Gran says that they actually have a lot in common."

"So Vivian is never going into the light?"

"Gran is working on her. She says that she's been telling Vivian that never going across isn't really an option, but then Edward comes over to visit and tells her something completely different."

"Are you and Edward speaking again?"

"No, and I'm not in a hurry to. I assume at some point he'll apologize and I'll forgive him but right now I don't need the stress in my life. I could use some good news right about now."

Wait, I had good news.

"I was going to call but I didn't want to bother you. Terrence said that my grandma talked about objects with energy and power. She hid them in the tunnel."

Why was I blurting this out? This was clearly not the time for this. But I knew that Missy would want to know.

Her eyes widened and she began to smile. I realized I hadn't seen her truly smiling since before Vivian's death.

"Oh my gosh, Tedi, that's amazing. We have to go down there and search. Have you told Jack yet?"

"I was going to when I got the three-alarm call to come back here."

Missy's smile grew wider and her gaze shifted to the door behind me. "It's like he has some sort of ESP power. He's always where he needs to be."

He was of course Jack, and Missy was correct. He did always seem to be just where we needed him to be. Before I could even greet him, he had the group quieted down and orderly.

"Tedi, can we use your drawing room for the reading of the will?"

"Of course, Jack."

I didn't have a chance to tell him that Vivian and Lane were in that room as well but I figured he'd see it for himself.

Everyone was gathered together. Missy, Dylan, his mother and father, Grandma Lane (although no one could see her), Herschel, Bandy, Alvin, Sadie, and the various aunts, uncles, and cousins. There was another person hovering in the doorway and I was surprised to see Andrea sort of waving at me. She was scheduled to check out today and I assumed she'd already left. I ducked out of the drawing room to see what she needed.

Today she was wearing a zebra striped blouse with flowered trousers in turquoise. She made an impact when she walked into a room.

"Tedi, I'm so glad to see you. I was hoping I could ask you if I could stay a few more days after all. They hired me to put together the post-funeral reception for Ms. Dashwood."

It was fine. Andrea could have checked with the front desk but she was definitely one of those "I'd like to speak to the manager" types from what I'd seen.

"Sure, just tell the person at the front desk that I said it was okay. I thought you had other clients to deal with though?"

Grimacing, Andrea shrugged. "I guess word has already got out about the wedding and the death. My client canceled on me. Getting the funeral reception was actually a godsend, and since I was already here I was able to give them a good price."

Sometimes things just work out. It looked like a win-win for both sides. I really did feel badly about my poor attitude about Andrea. She had only been doing her job, and she'd done it well. Until the murder.

She hurried away and I wasn't sure what I should do. I

wasn't family so there was no reason to be present for the reading of the will. On the other hand, they were in my drawing room and I was…well…curious.

It was clear that Jack didn't plan to leave them alone. He was sticking around, leaning against the wall and just watching what was going on. His presence made sense though. Whatever was in the will might be a motive for murder.

Everyone had found a seat or a place to stand. The attorney was unpacking his briefcase, and Lane and Vivian were standing in the back corner of the room just opposite of Jack. The invisible ladies were talking to one another but I couldn't hear what they were saying. Probably because of the spell.

In fact, the attorney appeared ready to begin and it seemed like everyone's gaze had turned to me. It looked like I wasn't wanted here.

"Let me know if you need anything," I said, rather too loudly. "I'll be in my office."

Except that I wasn't going to my office. I was heading straight into my closet on the other side of the wall. Did Herschel and Bandy have even more motive for murder? Had they hit the jackpot with Vivian's death?

We were about to find out.

IT ONLY TOOK a minute to leave the drawing room and head into my apartment's closet. I slipped in quietly, not wanting anyone to realize that there was a person on the other side of the wall.

The Ravenmist Inn was over a hundred and fifty years old. In that amount of time there had been numerous renovations and additions. At the main inn my apartment had been added to the first floor, so what was once an outside window and wall of my drawing room was now part of my walk-in closet. My grandmother had hung closed drapes over the walled-off window and had never given it a second thought. Now it came in handy when I wanted to eavesdrop on Jack and his suspects.

I settled on top of a large suitcase and leaned my ear against the wall of my closet, but I didn't really need to as the window was open enough to hear. The attorney had introduced himself as Arthur Bainbridge, Vivian's personal lawyer. He did the usual pre-will reading stuff, talking about when the will had been executed – which was a shock – because it had only been a few weeks ago. There had been a few audible gasps at that announcement. He also did the whole Vivian Dashwood was of sound mind and body stuff. Then he said that she had recorded herself reading the will.

Dramatic much?

Although it fit her personality perfectly. From what I'd seen and heard Vivian Dashwood loved the drama, especially if she was the one dishing it out.

From my vantage point, I had no idea what kind of recording Vivian had made or how Arthur Bainbridge was playing it. Perhaps on his phone? All I knew was that I could hear Vivian's voice stating her name and the date before she dove into how she was going to allocate her assets.

There was a list of about a half a dozen animal and children's charities with five figure bequests. I had to say that I was impressed with her generosity. She'd chosen a few of my favorites.

Then the fun started.

"To my faithful and hardworking assistant Sadie, I leave the sum of one hundred thousand dollars. She's made the last years so much easier on me."

Nice payday for Sadie. I'm sure she'd earned it.

"To Marian and Howard Carlisle, I leave the sum of five hundred thousand dollars. They've been good friends to me and never asked me for any financial help."

Marian and Howard were Dylan's parents. Good for them.

"To my brother-in-law Herschel Dashwood, I leave the sum of one dollar. He knows why, and in fact, the entire family knows why. I've given him close to a million dollars to help him with his half-witted business and get rich quick schemes so he's already gotten his share."

I heard some choking and coughing on the other side of the wall, plus the sound of chairs being scraped against my maple flooring.

"To my nephew Bandy, I leave the sum of one dollar. He also knows why. He's received more money from me than I can count and has done absolutely nothing with his worthless life. He inherited all of Herschel's worst traits and then added a few new ones."

Ouch, now that's gotta hurt.

"To my nephew Alvin, I leave the remaining fifty percent of my estate which includes my homes, cars, cash, stocks and bonds, plus the copyrights and royalties of my books. Unlike most of my family, Alvin has never asked me for a dime and has worked hard his entire life."

Whoa, Alvin.

"And last but certainly not least, to my great-nephew Dylan I leave the other fifty percent of my remaining estate. He's certainly worked hard and is his own man. I tried to discourage him from marrying his true love Missy but he never backed down. I was testing him and he passed with flying colors. I hope their marriage is long and happy, and I hope this money will alleviate the day to day worries a young couple might have."

Holy cow! My best friend was now filthy stinking rich. I didn't see that coming. Wow.

I was still in a state of disbelief when I heard the fracas start. Yelling, the sound of more chairs being scraped against my over a hundred-year-old restored maple floor, and then the sound of Jack telling everyone to calm down.

And I couldn't see any of it. Life isn't fair.

"You knew," I heard Bandy shout. "You knew about Vivian's will and you killed her for her money. You're a murderer."

"I didn't kill her," Alvin said, his own voice even louder. "I would never do something like that. I never cared about the money."

"That's a lie," Bandy said. "You've always cared. You had Vivian fooled. What happened? Could you not wait for her to die from natural causes anymore?"

"I'm going to sue," Herschel said, huffing and puffing. He sounded like he'd run a marathon. "I'm going to sue and set this will aside. Obviously, Vivian wasn't in her right mind when she wrote it."

There was a loud clearing of the throat before Arthur Bainbridge spoke.

"Vivian expected this sort of reaction. I can assure you that the will is airtight. She left you one dollar so that you couldn't claim that she had inadvertently left you out. She also sought the help of a doctor who signed off on her mental health before writing this will. You can sue but you'll be wasting your time and money."

There was a lot of muttering on the other side of the wall, and I imagined some gnashing of teeth as well.

Herschel and Bandy were not happy. I doubted they were going to give up easily. They didn't seem the type.

One thing was for sure...Vivian knew how to throw the drama around. But we still weren't any closer to finding her killer.

WHEN I EXITED my closet Lane and Vivian were standing in my living room, which startled me for a moment. I hadn't expected them to be there, but I probably should have. Vivian had a big smile on her face, almost like a child after being offered unlimited ice cream. Lane, on the other hand, looked rather sad.

"I'm really disappointed in you, Viv," Lane scolded her new friend and temporary roommate. "What you did wasn't kind. It probably isn't Bandy's fault that he's such a loser. Personally, I'd blame his parents."

"I do blame them, but Bandy has to take some of the responsibility himself. I've talked to him until I'm blue in the face from the time he was sixteen until about five years ago when I just gave up. I kept telling him that he needed to work harder, do better, but he's just like his father. They're always looking for a shortcut, mostly with my money. They got what they deserved if you ask me." Vivian seemed to suddenly notice that I was standing there. "What do you think? Do you think they deserve it?"

I had opinions but honestly, I didn't know any of these people very well.

"I don't know all of the family history involved here so I don't think I'll opine on this subject."

Vivian grunted and shook her head. "You sound like a politician. Trust me. They don't deserve a dime."

"And Alvin and Dylan do?" Lane asked. "I'm guessing they were much nicer to you."

"They never asked me for anything. I thought about leaving every penny to charity but then I realized it would make Herschel and Bandy even more angry if they saw their own family with the money. That would really make it hurt."

So it wasn't so much that Alvin and Dylan deserved millions but that Herschel and Bandy deserved a knife in the back. Revenge and all that jazz. It wasn't a pretty sight.

"Yet you're positive that Herschel would never kill you?"

The question just popped out of my mouth. I swear I didn't plan it.

Vivian's brows rose. "Yes, I am. He's always loved me, and he was counting on me to still have some love left for him at the end of my life. He miscalculated."

Stone cold. I had to hand it to Vivian, she wasn't backing down at all. No regrets.

I didn't know what to reply and luckily, I didn't have to. Missy rushed in, looking more than a little flustered.

"It's crazy in there," she said, pointing to the wall between the two rooms. "Jack is holding back Bandy. He tried to punch Alvin. Herschel is saying that this is somehow my fault and he's going to sue me personally for everything I have. I don't have anything but my Corolla and the bookstore."

Missy had always lived a quiet and frugal life. Her 2009 Corolla was in great shape due to regular maintenance, and the bookstore had been inherited from a close relative as Missy would need a cover to hide the fact that she was the Grim Reaper.

Vivian clapped her hands together and almost jumped up and down with glee.

"That's wonderful. I hope Alvin hits him back even harder."

I had furniture in that drawing room that was over a hundred years old and had been lovingly restored by hand. The last thing I needed was blood on the damask fabric. In fact, I was rapidly losing patience with Vivian. She'd had her revenge and now she needed to chill.

"Do you mind?" I asked sharply, turning my attention to the older woman. She was beginning to dim as she'd spent a great deal of her energy today. "I don't need my inn busted up for your entertainment."

"I'll pay for anything they break," she said with an air of disdain.

Except that Vivian didn't have any money anymore. She was dead. I didn't say it out loud though, because I'd been told by Missy that the newly passed on were often a tad sensitive about their status.

"I'd just rather avoid an altercation," I said instead. "It will be easier for us all."

"Tedi, we need to talk to Jack," Lane said. "I could tell that he wants to talk to us just by how he was looking at us in the drawing room. Can you tell him we're in here?"

"Sure, but knowing Jack—"

I didn't get any further. Jack sailed into my apartment, not even bothering to knock. I swear when the pressure is on around here, everyone forgets their manners. What if I'd decided to become a nudist? Not that I would, but I could have. I don't have wicker furniture or anything.

Jack barely spared me a glance. "Vivian, we need to talk."

Oh goody, Jack wasn't a happy camper. What else was new?

And I still hadn't told him about the tunnel yet. It probably wasn't a good time for a chat.

Chapter Ten

THERE WASN'T ANYTHING I could do to help Jack – or that he would allow me to do – so my mother, Daisy, and I slipped away and headed into the tunnel underneath the inn. I'd wanted Jack to go with us but he was busy at the moment. Daisy and my mother had convinced me that we'd be careful. If my grandmother had touched the object, it had to be okay.

Few people knew that the barn was connected to the inn basement by a tunnel. Missy and I had played down there when we were kids and before we truly understood the meaning of the word *creepy*. Now I avoided the damp, musty tunnel as much as possible.

Until today.

Armed with the biggest flashlight I could find, I cautiously creeped through the dark entrance to the tunnel, the smell of fresh earth and dampness all around me. There were definitely critters down here as well. My mind knew it but the rest of me was trying to pretend that I was taking a leisurely stroll on a sunny day, maybe in a park or on the banks of the River Seine in Paris.

Daisy and my mother were on my heels, but somehow I'd been elected the "leader" of this expedition so I was up front. If a bat or some other animal came for us, I'd be the first to get it.

That's some motherly love. Thanks, Mom.

When I was a kid I'd heard my mother say several times that she would gladly die for us. I couldn't help but wonder if maybe she'd changed her mind now that she'd seen how we'd all turned out as adults.

I heard frantic footsteps behind us and we all three whirled around to see Missy, holding her own flashlight.

"I came as fast as I could," she said, panting from her exertion. "I want to come with you."

I pointed to the ceiling which was, of course, the floor to the inn. "Shouldn't you be up there dealing with being a millionaire?"

"Dylan is talking to his family, and frankly, it's getting ugly. A lot of name calling and nastiness. Dylan told me to save myself and go. He'll deal with it all."

"I will never understand people. Do they think that being mean to you is going to make you want to share your windfall? It doesn't make any sense."

"People don't make much sense," Daisy countered. "I work with the public every day, so trust me on this."

"I'm glad that Dylan isn't going to allow his uncle to berate you, dear," Peggy said. "He needs to deal with his family."

Missy sighed. "I'm not even sure that I want the money. I mean…it's going to complicate everything. We have a nice, quiet but comfortable life and now it's all chaos. Will Dylan need to become a businessman? Will I have to give up the bookstore and my reaper duties? Are people always going to be coming to us for money? Because that doesn't sound like a good thing. And you know that I have a hard time saying no to anyone. I think Dylan is afraid that I'll just say yes and give it all away."

"So he's on board with having the money?" I asked.

Missy pressed her hands against her cheeks. "It looks like he is. We've been wealthy less than two hours and he's acting like an entirely different person to the one I ate breakfast with this morning. It's so weird. I think he's really happy about the money and he's already thinking of ways to spend it."

"Money changes people," Daisy said. "But I'm sure it will be fine. It's just all new and sort of exciting. So many opportunities that you didn't have before. He'll calm down soon."

"I agree," my mother said. "He's just in shock. It will all be fine."

Was Dylan changing? I didn't like the sound of this. Missy and Dylan had known one another for years, though. He was probably just in shock, like my mother said.

"We need to get to work," Peggy said. "And remember, if you see something don't touch it."

With me leading the pack, we inched our way down the tunnel in an excruciatingly slow manner. We didn't know what we were really looking for so it made the job even harder. If it was buried, we'd be out of luck unless my grandmother had drawn a big X where she'd hidden it. That would be nice but far-fetched. I'd been down here more times than I could count and I'd never seen anything like that.

I'd spent quite a bit of time last night trying to remember what I had seen as a child. My memories were still rather vivid, Missy and I playing tag and hide and go seek in the dark tunnel. My grandmother hadn't thought twice about letting us run around down here so I don't think she thought that we could get into any danger, although I was brought up in a time before bicycle helmets and five-point harnesses for kids in cars. Childhood had been more of a Darwin experiment back then and with my grandmother even more so. She didn't baby a skinned knee or bruise. She'd just tell me to tough it out and walk it off.

We'd come to the end and the ladder that would take us into the old barn on the property. I was feeling defeated since we'd found absolutely nothing. I'd been so sure that Terrence's information would be the break we'd been waiting for. I should have known it wouldn't be as easy as a stroll down a dark tunnel.

"Now what?" Daisy asked.

"That's a very good question," Peggy said, turning this way and that with her flashlight. "I didn't see anything the entire time. Tedi, are you sure Terrence said the tunnel? Maybe Grandma Rose was confused."

"Grandma Rose was sharp as a tack until the day she passed," I replied. "We should all be that lucky and have that amazing of a memory. If she said the tunnel, then it's the tunnel."

"Then maybe Terrence misheard," Missy said. "What word sounds like tunnel?"

Is there a word that rhymes with *tunnel*? Funnel? Was there a *funnel* in Ravenmist?

"He seemed very sure," I said. "I don't think he could have confused a tunnel with something else."

"You're in the wrong tunnel."

"Uh…was that a strange voice?"

"Mom, did you just speak?"

"No, dear. It wasn't me."

"It wasn't me," Daisy said.

"It wasn't me either," Missy echoed.

And it wasn't me. That meant we had some company. The biggest question for me wasn't *who was it* but *how long had they been watching and following us*?

"Um, hello. Hello? Can you show yourself?"

A whoosh of air ran over my already chilled skin and then a man stood a few feet from us. He was dressed in overalls and heavy boots, his dark hair a little long and messy. I was terrible with ages but I put his at somewhere around forty, give or take five years.

"Hello," I said again. I was used to meeting spirits now, but I was a little nervous. Not all ghosts were nice and kind. It all depended on how they were in life. "My name is Tedi. This is Missy, Daisy, and my mother Peggy."

He didn't answer at first, sort of taking stock of us before answering.

"I'm Edgar," he finally said. "I haven't seen you down here for a long time."

The last time was when I was escaping the press when a movie star had been murdered in Ravenmist. Before that? Literally years.

"How long have you been down here?"

"I don't know. What year is it?"

I told him and he seemed surprised. I'd heard that time passes differently in the in-between.

"I've been down here since 1886. I watch over the tunnels."

That sounded like an important job.

Missy stepped forward. "You said we were in the wrong tunnel. But this is the only tunnel that we know of."

"There's another tunnel from the barn to an old storage shed, and a third from the inn to a demolished guest house. There may be others that I don't know about."

"Are you sure?" I asked. "I've never heard about those tunnels. Mom, what about you?"

Peggy shook her head. "I haven't either."

Edgar scowled but not in a mean way, more frustrated with me. "I should know. I helped dig those tunnels. I worked here at the inn doing odd jobs, and I remember Rose. A good woman. I remember her hiding something. She told me she was afraid of it and that I should stay away from it too."

Score.

"Then you know where it is?" I asked excitedly. "Do you know what it is?"

He shook his head. "She never showed it to me. She just said to stay away from it. I don't think you should be going near it either."

I didn't want to argue with a ghost.

"We really need to find it. There are...evil forces that may be looking for it. We need to get to it first."

I didn't go into detail, and I didn't want to. We'd kept a great deal of the situation on the down-low; the only spirit in on all the secrets was Terrence. Because he lived with me and it would be difficult for him not to know. I trusted him. He was aware that if everyone in Ravenmist knew that there might be mass fear and hysteria. No one wanted that.

Edgar appeared conflicted but eventually nodded his head. "I really liked Rose. She was a good person. She was always nice to me."

My grandmother had been the best. I still missed her. She always had time to talk and she made the best cheesecake this side of the Mississippi. Maybe the other side too.

He pointed to the ladder and then disappeared, leaving us to climb up to the barn like the humans we were. He was waiting for us when we got there, leading us to the tool room in the big barn. This was a building that was mostly used for storage now.

The tool room was an actively used part of the structure where maintenance kept their equipment. I hadn't been in this room often, to be honest. It wasn't huge, maybe ten by ten, but it was one area that was organized and well-kept.

"Is the tunnel in here?" my mother asked. "I don't see anything."

I didn't either. Everything looked normal.

"It's here. You have to concentrate on the floor," Edgar said. "It's hidden with magic."

Magic, again? This was getting tiresome. What else couldn't I see because of some spell?

We all stared down at the floor and…nothing. Nada. I was getting impatient when Missy decided to take a step forward, waving her hand over the weathered concrete.

Presto.

Maybe because she was a supernatural being, the floor immediately blurred and then a trapdoor showed itself.

Well…that was interesting. I wanted to know how many of those suckers were all over Ravenmist.

"Where does it lead?" Daisy asked, cautiously lifting the wooden door. "Is the object down here?"

Edgar shook his head. "No, it's in the tunnel the goes from the inn to the old guest house. This tunnel goes to an old storage shed by the pond."

I knew that shed. Or had known it. It had collapsed during a terrible thunderstorm a few years ago. The winds had been frightening and the structure rickety. It was now a pile of old wood.

"And you're saying that there's another tunnel out of the inn? Will you show us?" I asked.

"I'll meet you in the drawing room," Edgar replied, grabbing a crowbar from the wall of tools before fading away again.

The drawing room? I'd been in that room a million times. I'd never seen anything there. More magic?

We trudged back through the tunnel to the inn, gathering in the drawing room. Once again, I didn't see anything.

Edgar appeared and walked over to a decorative rug in front of a large window, picking it up and setting it aside. There was no trapdoor underneath, however.

"Do we have to concentrate again?" I asked with a sigh.

Edgar frowned and began to pry up my prized maple flooring with the crowbar. What the heck...?

"No, it's under these floorboards."

And it was. Before I could yell at him for ruining my floor he'd uncovered a round hole that I had never in my entire life realized even existed. And I'd been over pretty much every inch of this inn and its grounds.

"There was a hole in the floor all this time," Daisy marveled. "I never would have guessed. Why on earth was it dug in the first place?"

Edgar just smiled mysteriously. "There was a lot going on here back then."

Okie dokey. Edgar didn't elaborate and frankly, with everything going on I was afraid to even ask what he meant. It was a long time ago and did it really matter now? Probably not.

One by one, we climbed down into the dark tunnel following its twists and turns until it felt like we were beginning to climb up a bit. Missy was once again in the lead and she pushed open the door at the other end, all of us scrambling out of the tunnel and into the old cellar of the guest house.

The small room had been used for storage back in the day, keeping vegetables cool below ground before modern refrigeration existed. There wasn't much left, except a pile of rotted wood and a large stone structure built into the walls, almost like a cabinet but without doors. Pieces of it had fallen and broken, creating a mound of debri right at the opening.

I'd been at the old guest house years ago when I was a kid. Missy and I ran all of this property in the summer, only returning to the inn when we were hungry or the weather was bad. The structure had crumbled into nothing before I was even born.

Daisy pushed at the rotted wood pile to our left with her foot. Nothing underneath. It only left one other option. My mother stepped in front of the stone cabinet but Missy grabbed her arm.

"If the object is there, it could be harmful to a human. Let me look for it."

She had a point. As a supernatural being, Missy might have more protection.

The stone cabinet was large but the opening wasn't. Luckily, Missy was able to actually crawl into it but she had little room to spare. We heard her moving around but could only see her legs sticking out. After what seemed like an eternity, she began to back out.

"I found something. It was really wedged in there between the stones. I had to work to get it out."

She stood and I could see what looked like a burlap sack with a bulky item inside of it. She stepped away from the cabinet but must have caught her shoe on one of the stones because she pitched forward, the object flying out of her hands. Daisy was close by and grabbed Missy before she could fall to the ground but she couldn't catch the sack as well.

It was pure instinct. I didn't have time to think it through.

My hands reached out and the sack landed in them. Safe and sound.

Everyone seemed to suck in their breath, their eyes wide – including me – as we waited to see if I would shrivel up and die or maybe explode into a million little pieces.

Nothing happened.

"Oh my stars," Missy exclaimed, straightening up and dusting off her clothes. "You might have been killed. Or worse. We don't know what that thing does."

I gingerly held onto the sack, keeping it at arm's length. "I was afraid to let it fall to the ground. What if we broke it?"

"What if we broke you?" my mother said, still breathless from the incident. "Tedi, you need to be more careful."

"I didn't really think it through. I just grabbed it."

"Well, give it to me," Missy said brusquely. "We don't need to tempt fate here."

I happily handed it over and was quite relieved when it was out of my possession.

Missy knelt on the ground and opened the sack. "So let's see what we've found."

A brass bowl, green from all the years it had sat there. Just a plain bowl, about the size I'd make cereal in but it did have some scrolls and circles engraved on it. It didn't look special or magical in the least.

Did it even have power? And if it did, what kind?

Chapter Eleven

JACK WAS LIVID. Beyond angry. Even apple pie couldn't calm him down. I had never seen him like this before. It was almost as if he couldn't find the words to express just how mad he was, then he would and they'd all come out in a rush before he'd clam up again, simply pacing around the middle of my living room.

He stopped abruptly, his cheeks still a ruddy shade. "You could have been killed. Or seriously hurt. None of you have a clue as to what you're digging into. Not a clue."

Now that hurt a little. I had been trying to help. Heck, I'd visited Hell with Missy. Not many people had visited Hell and come back to talk about it.

"I didn't touch it on purpose," I repeated. I'd told him the story twice but he didn't seem to be calming down at all. "Missy was falling. I didn't know what was in the sack. It might have broken. It was just instinct that made me grab it."

"That instinct could have gotten you killed, Tedi."

I took a deep breath and tried to count to ten. I got to four. "I agree that it's not the smartest thing I've ever done, but can we all be glad that nothing bad happened? It's okay, Jack."

"This time." He started pacing again. "This is becoming a pattern, Tedi, and it needs to stop. You're going to get hurt or killed. You need to stay out of my investigations and you really need to stay out of the supernatural world. You're completely defenseless."

I knew that. But...

"I can't just sit idly by and watch humanity be wiped from the earth. I have to do something."

He stopped again, his expression thunderous. "Do you not trust me? I can handle this. I don't need your help. It was one thing to have you doing some research. That was fine, but going to search for it on your own? That's insanity, and I'm not going to pretend that it's any different. I'll tell Daisy, Missy, and your mother the same thing. Do you not have even a shred of self-preservation? Not an inkling? You're like a lamb trotting happily to their own slaughter."

An image of me in a lamb's costume whistling a happy tune ran through my mind. I couldn't help but sort of laugh, which was exactly the wrong thing to do at that moment.

"Are you laughing at me, Tedi?"

Absolutely not. That would be bad.

"It was the image," I tried to explain. "Me looking like a lamb. It is kind of funny."

Apparently, Jack didn't think so. If anything, he looked even angrier and I was the reason.

"Jack, I'm sorry. I can't be any sorrier. I can't keep saying it over and over. I mean...I guess I can, but at some point the apology is going to lose its meaning. I'm just sorry, okay? I am trying to be careful, but you've been busy with the case–"

Jack whirled around. "Don't put this on me. If you'd told me, I would have made time. You just wanted to do it, and you didn't want to wait."

It was beginning to dawn on me that Jack and I were having our first fight as a couple. I vaguely recognized it though as my ex and I hadn't spent much of our marriage arguing. David didn't believe in fighting. He said it was a waste of time. Instead he just did whatever he wanted and ignored me when I was mad. I once followed him around our condo for almost an hour trying to get him to talk to me but he kept going into another room. Eventually, he'd grabbed his car keys and went for a drive. So I could *cool down.* I'm still mad about that.

"It was my grandmother that put it there, Jack. She obviously touched it and it didn't hurt her. She was fine."

"We don't know that your grandmother didn't put any spells or charms on it to protect it. If she had you could have been seriously hurt."

"My grandmother wasn't a witch."

Although the spell that kept the trapdoor invisible in the tool room had to have come from somewhere.

"My grandmother wasn't a witch," I repeated. "I never saw anything to indicate that. I would know if she had been."

Right? Except that I didn't know that Missy was the Grim Reaper for literally years and years.

"Your friends and mother have been known to cast a spell or two on occasion. Maybe your grandmother had a friend help her. We don't know what happened back then. But I do know that some of these supernatural artifacts can be deadly."

"I–"

But Jack wasn't done.

"We also have no idea if Orien or any other evil demon can feel this object being lifted from its resting place. Or just feel a surge in power around him in general. So far, we've been lucky and Orien has kept to himself. But you might have made the situation much worse, Tedi. You could have alerted Orien to what we're doing. If I'd known you were going to look for it, I would have made sure to put a net of protection over you so he couldn't sense your actions. Now I have no idea what he knows. You've endangered everyone in Ravenmist with your foolishness."

Oh. That was bad. I hadn't thought about that. Daisy, Missy, and Mom hadn't either. The last thing we wanted to do was make more trouble.

"I'm so sorry, Jack. I swear we were just trying to help."

I was fighting back tears now at the thought of killing my fellow townsfolk when what I was really trying to do was help them. I had messed this up big time.

"I'm sorry," I said again. I really, really meant it too.

Jack rubbed the back of his neck. I had a terrible feeling I'd put a pain there.

"You have to think before you act, Tedi. We're fighting

something bigger and stronger than you can even imagine. One wrong step and it's all over."

All I could do is say that I was sorry. Again. It sounded weak and lame to my own ears so I could only imagine how it sounded to him.

"How is the case coming? Have you made progress?"

I desperately wanted to change the subject.

Jack sighed heavily. "It's pretty much the same. Everyone hated Vivian so they all have a motive. Herschel and Bandy are in some deep financial trouble. I did find that out from my friend who is combing through backgrounds. So far, they have the biggest motive assuming they thought they were going to inherit. Alvin and Dylan seem shocked that they inherited so much but I still need to look into them too."

"What about Sadie?"

"As far as I can tell, she didn't have any motive other than hating her job and despising Vivian. But if Vivian was dead, then she wouldn't have a job anymore. The attorney said that Sadie didn't have any knowledge that she was being left money in the will."

"Zack, Dylan's best man, argued with Herschel the night before the wedding."

"I talked to him and he said that he did argue with Herschel about a business deal. Herschel wanted Zack to invest in the nightclub and Zack just laughed at him. He didn't even have any negative contact with Vivian so he's not a suspect either."

That left Herschel and Bandy.

Jack's phone buzzed and he pulled it out of his pocket to check it.

"I have to go. Try not to get killed while I'm gone."

That was plan B, actually. Plan A was not to get *all of* humanity killed.

Jack stomped out, leaving me standing in the middle of my own living room, replaying our heated conversation over and over in my head. I'd messed up badly. I'd apologized. I couldn't do much more than that. I'd had good intentions.

And we all know what the road to Hell is paved with…

I felt horrible. I'd screwed up royally and I didn't have any way to fix it.

I needed pie. Immediately.

The Grateful Raven, here I come.

THE SUNSHINE AND warm weather didn't help my mood at all. I'd made a huge mistake and Jack was right. Saying sorry wouldn't fix it. If Orien knew that we'd found a powerful object…

I was halfway to the diner when I saw Alvin and Andrea standing on the sidewalk talking. Actually, it looked like Alvin was doing the talking and she was doing the listening part. She was nodding, her expression serious. I remembered that they'd known each other long before the wedding. Andrea had worked for Alvin previously.

He waved, giving me a big smile. "Tedi, how are you today?"

"I'm fine, thank you. How are you?"

"Just finishing up some final details for Vivian's service with Andrea. She's doing a great job."

"I'm trying to do my best," Andrea said. "And that means that I do need to get back to work. Alvin, let me know if you need anything else. Tedi, it was lovely to see you today."

"It was good to see you too."

Andrea headed back down the sidewalk, leaving me and Alvin standing under the shade of a large oak tree.

"She's a hard worker," Alvin said as he watched her walk away. "I have total confidence that the service will be just what Vivian would have wanted."

I didn't tell him that he could simply go by Grandma Lane's house and ask Vivian what she wanted. I still had hopes that she would cross over but with every day that passed that hope was growing dimmer.

"I'm sure it will be."

Alvin turned his attention back to me. "I hope that you'll let Missy know that I'm so sorry that she's caught up in my family's drama. Vivian loved the drama, you see. She loved to stir the pot and see what happened. I think I was the only one that truly understood Vivian. I wasn't a huge fan of her drama-inducing antics but that's just who she was. I tried to meet her where she stood instead of trying to drag her into being someone she wasn't. I never tried to change her and I think she appreciated that about me. She was all about her career. Telling stories was the only thing she ever wanted to do."

"She was hugely successful at that."

"I want you to know that I never asked her for money. Not like the others in the family. But I'd like to think that if I had, she would have given it to me because she genuinely liked me. She knew I wouldn't ask unless I was totally desperate and destitute. I wasn't out looking for a quick buck."

I wasn't sure how to respond. I had no clue if Vivian would have given him the money or not. And if she had, would she have taken him out of her will? Luckily, it didn't appear that Alvin was looking for me to say anything. He seemed off in his own world talking about his aunt. I did feel sorry for him. He seemed to have genuine feelings for her.

"No one could tell a better story than Vivian," he went on. "I knew most of them weren't real but they were so entertaining that I'd listen anyway. You know, she liked to pretend that she was this big New York City socialite with lots of rich and influential friends but that really wasn't the case. She mostly worked. Sometimes twelve to fourteen hours a day for weeks if she was on a deadline. They had a few good friends but they mostly drifted away over the years. Not too many people could deal with Vivian and her high-strung personality. They'd get tired of it eventually."

I still didn't know what to say. This was...awkward.

"It's good that she had you then."

Alvin shook his head. "My dad and brother could never understand. They didn't have the patience. I'd like to think that they didn't do this heinous act but they've constantly surprised me with their greed."

I sucked in a breath. "Do you think that they…?"

"I don't know," he said with a shake of his head. "I do know that if they did, it wasn't planned ahead or anything. Maybe they were arguing and it got heated."

"Vivian was hit from behind," I pointed out. "She wasn't face to face and arguing with her attacker."

"Maybe they argued earlier or she thought they were done arguing. I just don't think that my dad or brother would kill in cold blood."

This was interesting. Alvin actually thought that Herschel or Bandy could be a killer. I sure had issues with my sisters now and again but I'd never thought that one of them might get angry enough to murder someone.

"Where were you right before the bouquet toss?" I asked him. I was trying to picture the reception but I couldn't remember where he was.

"I was at my table watching the dancing," Alvin said. "I'm not much of a dancer but I enjoy the music."

Should I tell Jack that Alvin thought his father and brother might have done it? Did he already know? Would he care?

Except that Jack wasn't really speaking to me at the moment. I'd been planning to drown my sorrows in a coconut meringue pie. First, a slice of pie. Then maybe I'd talk to Jack.

If he wanted to talk to me, that is.

Chapter Twelve

I MUST HAVE looked about as miserable as I felt because Daisy took one look at me and bundled me into a booth with a huge slab of pie and a cup of coffee. I silently ate about half of it before I could tell her my tale of woe.

"Jack hates me."

Daisy didn't even seem all that shocked. Was I that much of a menace?

"I'm sure that he doesn't hate you. He's probably just upset. What did you do?"

"Maybe I didn't do anything. Maybe he did something and won't admit it. Why does this have to be my fault?"

"Because of the look on your face when you got here. You know it's something you did."

Sighing, I rubbed at my temple. "I told Jack about touching the bowl. He went ballistic. Totally exploded. He said we shouldn't have gone searching alone and that we could have been killed by the object. He also said that Orien might be able to feel the shift in the universe's energy when we moved it. We might have set the evil demons off and they'll come and slaughter all of mankind because we were stupid."

Daisy's eyes were wide and I saw her swallow hard. "So he's mad at all of us, not just you?"

"Yes, but I was the one that had to hear about it. He went on and on and on... When he finally left I felt about an inch tall. What if we've sentenced mankind to death, Daisy? I don't think I could live with myself if I did that."

"No one would be living with that," Daisy pointed out. "Does he really think that we did? We were just trying to help."

"That's what I told him. He was unmoved by my plea. I said I'm sorry about a hundred times. What else can I do? I can't turn back time and make it not happen."

With a loud thud, a giant book dropped onto the middle of the table. Missy was the dropper.

"Actually, you might be able to," she said, sliding into the booth next to me.

"Be able to what?"

"Turn back time."

"If I could do that, I would have done it long before now."

Missy didn't reply, instead opening the dusty book and pointed to the illustration on the page. "There. Do you see it? It's the bowl that we found."

Daisy and I leaned over the yellowed page. The drawing definitely looked like the bowl that we'd found but I couldn't understand a word that was written in the book. It was in a language I didn't speak or read.

"Is this Greek or Latin?" Daisy asked, squinting at the tiny print. "I can't make it out."

"It's an old language used by those with supernatural power. It's not something you can learn in school," Missy explained.

I picked up my fork and took another bite of the sweet creation in front of me. I had a feeling I was going to need the sugar. "What does it say?"

"It says that the bowl can be used for moving back and forth in time."

"How?"

"It doesn't say how. It just says that we can."

I wasn't sure how this was going to help us in the fight between good and evil. Perhaps we could go way back in the very beginning and stop the battle from even beginning at all.

"I need to take this to Jack. If he'll talk to me."

Daisy tapped the book. "He'll talk to you if you have this. Just say you're sorry again."

Missy frowned. "Did I miss something? What are you sorry for? What did you do, Tedi?"

Rolling my eyes, I took one more bite of my pie. "Actually, it's what we all did that he's angry about. I'm just the one getting the heat for it. By the way, have you talked to Vivian yet? Now that she's had her revenge on her family is she ready to cross over?"

Sighing, Missy shook her head. "I don't think so. She and grandma are becoming really close friends. She may never cross over."

"Has Edward been visiting her?" Daisy asked.

"Not when I'm there."

Daisy and I exchanged a quick glance.

"Maybe…maybe you and Edward should bury the hatchet," I suggested.

Preferably, not in one another's back.

"He owes me an apology," Missy replied primly. "Until then I'm not budging."

I didn't push the subject. Edward had acted badly.

Besides, I couldn't afford to lose any more friends.

Had Jack cooled down yet? I was about to find out.

THE SUN WAS down when I arrived at Jack's house. There was a light on in the front window letting me know that he was home. I sat in my car for a few minutes giving myself a pep talk before ringing the doorbell. Even though I had something important to tell him, he still might not want to talk to me.

Reluctantly, I exited my vehicle, the heavy book tucked under my arm. The front door swung open and Jack stood there, his expression neutral. If he was happy or sad I had no idea, which I'm sure was what he wanted. He liked to play close to the vest, if you know what I mean.

"Tedi."

"Jack."

"I didn't expect to see you this evening."

I bet he didn't.

"I didn't either but then Missy brought me this book."

I held it up as he closed the front door behind me. The house was empty as Tyler was in Chicago with his mother. There was a half-eaten pizza on the kitchen counter, a brand from the grocery store. I recognized the empty box next to the stove. Now I really felt awful. Jack was reduced to eating frozen food for dinner when he could have been eating something fresh from my chef's kitchen.

I plopped the book onto the coffee table and opened it to the bookmarked page.

"It says that the bowl is a time travel object."

Jack leaned forward, studying the page.

"It doesn't say how that it does that, though."

He looked up at me, a smile playing on his lips. "I know, Tedi. I can read."

I was about to retort that it wasn't in any known language to humans but then I remembered that he was a demon.

Wait…he was almost smiling. He wasn't mad anymore.

"Am I out of the doghouse?"

"Yes, and I'm sorry I lost my temper. I just get worried about you. If something happened, I'd never forgive myself. I'm supposed to be here to protect all of you."

"I thought you moved here for Tyler."

"That was just a pleasant bonus. I'm here because I could feel the universe's rumblings. I *needed* to be here."

"What are the rumblings saying now? Did I awaken Orien?"

"I don't know yet."

"I am really sorry, Jack."

He exhaled slowly, his shoulders slumped. "I know, Tedi, and I'm sorry too. I don't like it when we argue. I know that you were trying to help, but I literally have the weight of humanity on my shoulders. It can, at times, make me grumpy."

"So will the bowl help?"

Jack stared down at the pages for a moment and then shrugged. "I have no idea how time travel would help us. I'll have to think on this. In the meantime, we need to keep it from Orien and his evil friends."

That. Right there.

"You say *we need* to do that as if you mean me and you and the others. But do you mean that? Because this is where I get confused. You say things like that and then I try to help and you get upset."

"I do want you to help. I just don't want you to get hurt."

That made two of us.

"I don't want to get hurt either. And I don't want *you* to get hurt."

Jack chuckled because apparently I'd said something very funny.

"I can heal quickly and I'm practically impossible to kill." He waggled his eyebrows. "So don't get any ideas about offing me. No matter how mad at me you are."

"I wasn't the one mad. You were. By the way, are you impressed by how I'm not getting involved in the investigation?"

"I was, but now I see that you were just busy searching for

supernatural relics."

I wanted to stick my tongue out at him but that was too immature. Even for me.

"How is the case going? Are Missy and Dylan close to being able to go on their honeymoon?"

Jack took two cans of soda from the fridge, opened them, and then handed one to me. I don't know how he knew but yes, I was thirsty.

"I need to talk to Dylan," Jack replied. "But for some reason he's been putting me off. I'm not sure why."

"He did just inherit millions. He might be a bit preoccupied."

"His inheritance is why I need to talk to him."

"Just talk to Missy. I'm sure they were pretty much inseparable all day. Where she was, he would be. Does Dylan need an alibi now? Even if I hated someone's guts, I don't think I'd kill them at my own wedding."

Jack sat on the beige couch, stretching out his legs, and I sat next to him. The complete lack of anything personal in this room never ceased to amaze me. I'd seen hotel rooms with more character.

"I did talk to Missy. She said she lost track of Dylan as they were making the rounds and talking to people. She assumed he went to the bathroom or to get a drink or something. She wasn't concerned about it. He showed up right before she was going to toss the bouquet."

"You really don't think Dylan did it, do you? He couldn't

have known he was going to inherit."

"I need to ask him that. According to Vivian, no one knew about her updated will but the lawyer might have let something slip. She can't be certain."

"I don't think she's ever going to cross over into the light. Missy said that Lane and Vivian are best pals now."

"When I was there, Edward was visiting as well."

My ears perked up. It was the first I was hearing about our ghost who had...ghosted us.

"No one has seen Edward. We're all a little worried."

"You don't need to worry about Edward. He's fine."

"He has no place to live—"

"He's fine," Jack repeated. "He showed up at the station and asked if he could stay there. I told him he could as long as he didn't get up to any funny stuff. I don't want people talking about the haunted sheriff's station. So far, it's been fine. He keeps to himself and doesn't make any trouble. I did have to tell him that I wasn't going to go to the bookstore for him to get him more books. I lent him my library card instead."

"Is he sorry?"

Jack shrugged. "Who knows? He does seem a little less...brash."

A subdued Edward? That would be interesting to see.

"Jack, who do you think killed Vivian? Is it Herschel and Bandy?"

"They do seem to be the most likely suspects."

"How do you prove it? They said they didn't do it."

"If there's something there, I'll find it."

I admired Jack's confidence. And patience. It seemed like there were several suspects with motive.

And absolutely no evidence. Where would he go from here?

Would the killer get away scot free?

Chapter Thirteen

JACK AND I were sitting in the dining room of the inn the next
morning, both of us enjoying a delicious breakfast. I was
having the pancakes and he was having a feast of bacon, eggs,
toast, and a bowl of oatmeal with strawberries. His favorite.

I was on my second cup of coffee when Missy rushed in,
tears running down her cheeks. My normally cool and calm
friend looked like she'd slept in her clothes...for about a week.
Her hair was sticking up in the back and her socks didn't match.

Something was terribly, awfully wrong.

Jack must have realized it too because he jumped up when I
did, rushing to her side to find out what was wrong so we could
immediately fix it. I'd never seen her like this before and to be
truthful it shook me to my core.

Missy held out a crumpled piece of paper. "He just left me
this note. He's gone."

I didn't know for sure who "he" was but I had an idea.

"Dylan left?" I asked, taking the paper and carefully unfold-
ing it. "Where did he go?"

"I don't know," Missy sobbed but much more quietly. I

think she'd realized she was in full view of several diners, including her new in-laws, Herschel, Bandy, and Alvin, who were eating breakfast on the other side of the dining room. "He doesn't say. He just says that he'll be in touch in a few days or weeks. Weeks? That's crazy."

A quick reading of the rather short note told me that Dylan needed to think about everything that had happened, including inheriting millions. He wanted some time away and would be in touch. In days or weeks. Frankly, I didn't blame Missy for being upset. One look at Jack's face told me he wasn't a happy camper either.

"This is strange timing," Jack said, a muscle jumping in his tight jaw. "But I can put a BOLO out for him. Don't worry, Missy, I'll find Dylan."

Jack was reaching for his cell phone when Alvin stood up from his chair, his hands wrapped around his own neck, gasping for air. He only stood for a few seconds though, crumpling to the floor in a heap, his face a bright reddish-purple.

I wasn't as fast as Jack was in getting to him but in the meantime, Herschel had grabbed one of those allergy pens out of Alvin's front shirt pocket and shoved it into his thigh. Immediately, Alvin began to breathe easier, his color going back to normal.

Jack was kneeling down next to him along with Herschel. For once, I had to admit that Herschel was the hero of the day. He'd clearly assessed the situation and known what to do.

I called emergency services and they showed up a few

minutes later, checking Alvin's vitals and making sure he didn't need to be transported to the hospital. He kept saying that he was fine, and he did look better, but Missy and I were both trying to convince him to go get checked out by a real doctor.

I did, however, have another concern. As an inn and restaurant owner I took allergies extremely seriously. I needed to know if we had caused this so I could try and make some sort of amends.

"Alvin, what are you allergic to?"

He took a gulp of water from his glass. "Strawberries. My only allergy is strawberries."

Strawberries?

I took a quick look at Alvin's meal and immediately saw the culprit. Two small strawberries shoved down into his oatmeal. He probably hadn't even noticed them when he took his first bite. Maybe even a second or third.

Now the oatmeal that the inn serves doesn't normally come with strawberries. You have to order them special like Jack does. Unless Alvin ordered the strawberries – and why would he – they shouldn't have been there. At all.

"Jack, I need to go check something in the kitchen."

I didn't waste any time, immediately questioning my cooks as to who made the oatmeal. The head chef wouldn't have done a simple bowl of oatmeal himself; one of the assistants would have made it. Craig, who had been with me for three years and had always done an excellent job, said that he was making the bowls of oatmeal this morning. He'd made several but only one with strawberries. He'd also made one with blueberries but the rest were plain.

When I questioned him further, really pressing his memory, he swore up and down that he'd only made one single bowl with strawberries. He'd known it was for the sheriff since it was his regular breakfast order, so he'd put in a few extra. A normal order of strawberries would be four to six, depending on size. He'd put in eight.

"By the way, Tedi, your friend Dylan was here not long ago looking for you," my head chef said when he had a break in his duties.

Dylan? In the excitement I'd completely forgotten that he was missing.

"Where is he?"

The chef shrugged. "I dunno. He came in here looking for you and then left, I guess. It was a madhouse in here and I didn't pay much attention to him. I guess he didn't find you."

He hadn't. But what had he been doing here in the first place? And why did he want to talk to me but not to Missy? It didn't make any sense.

I didn't realize that Jack had joined me in the kitchen until he asked the chef a question.

"Dylan was in the kitchen? Was he anywhere near the out-going food?"

Was Jack upset about the lack of a hair net?

"He walked through the kitchen and then back out so...I guess he was. Can I go back to work now?"

Jack said yes, which left me to ask him what he was up to.

"Why did you ask that?"

"Because Dylan had an opportunity to put strawberries in Alvin's oatmeal."

Wait…no.

"Dylan would never do that," I protested. "And don't let Missy hear you say that. She's upset enough already."

Jack's brows rose. "Dylan was here in the kitchen…

"To see me."

"Maybe. Then strawberries disappear from my oatmeal and land in Alvin's. Your staff would never do that. So…"

"No. Just no. Why would Dylan try to kill Alvin? It doesn't make any sense, Jack."

"Maybe he wants all of the money, not just half."

"There's no guarantee that he'd get Alvin's half."

"That's true, it would depend on how the will is written."

We were at a standoff. Neither one of us was going to budge.

"Dylan wouldn't do this," I repeated. "I'm sure there's a perfectly reasonable explanation for this."

"We should ask him. Oh wait, we can't because he's run off. Kind of suspicious, don't you think?"

I had to admit that the timing was bad. Not good. It didn't help my case.

"What about Herschel or Bandy? They might have done it."

"I did ask and it's a possibility. Alvin was in the men's room when the food was delivered to the table. No one has been ruled out yet."

I didn't know what to say at this point. When Jack gets like this it was like moving the Rock of Gibraltar. I wasn't going to win any arguments.

"I need to go back out there and make sure Alvin is okay and doesn't want to sue me. And I need to check on Missy."

"I need to go find Dylan. I have a few questions for him."

I had a few questions for Dylan myself. The first one?

What on earth were you thinking?

THE GOOD NEWS was that I wasn't going to be sued. Alvin assured me that he wasn't the litigious kind and that he wasn't upset or angry, looking for someone to blame. Just in case, I comped his entire stay at the inn which shocked the heck out of him. He declared that he would use the money he saved and give to a charity of my choosing. I'd always liked Alvin and I liked him even more now.

As for the bad news, I had to drag Missy into my apartment to calm her down and clean her up for the funeral reception that was scheduled to take place in the convention center in only a few hours. Jack had released the crime scene this morning in just enough time to get it set up and ready. There were going to be quite a few attendees – pretty much all of Dylan's family and then some of Missy's as well.

Andrea was everywhere this morning, bustling in and out of the kitchen and making the short trek to the convention center over and over so that every detail was taken care of. This time I didn't resent her role at all. Because she was handling the reception, I was able to spend time with Missy when she needed me the most.

"I'm going to yell at Dylan when I see him," she said, smoothing down the dress I'd lent her. Honestly, it looked better on her than me. We were sitting in my apartment relaxing until it was time to go to the reception. "And I'm going to make him listen until I'm done."

"No, you won't. You'll hug him. You'll be glad to see him."

Sighing, Missy nodded. "You're probably right, but I'm still mad at him."

"He must be under a great deal of pressure to do something like this. It's not like him at all."

It really wasn't. I liked Dylan and I didn't want to have to change my opinion of him if at all possible. He was a good guy and he made Missy happy.

Just not today. But they had a lifetime together ahead of them and there would be days like this no matter how much they loved each other. They were going to get on each other's nerves now and again.

We chatted for awhile, remembering about when we were younger and life seemed so much simpler. When we lived for summer vacation and were smarter than our parents.

Eventually it was time to go to the service and we headed for the parking lot. We had just stepped outside when I saw Jack approaching us.

Thank the heavens, he had Dylan with him.

Like something out of a romantic movie, Missy and Dylan ran into each other's arms, both of them babbling and kissing as if they hadn't seen one another in years. I got a little lump in my throat watching them reunite. If there was true love out there, this was it.

I was kinda sorta jealous.

I don't like to admit it but what the heck. Missy and Dylan had won at this love stuff. They were truly, madly, and deeply head over heels. We should all be so lucky.

"I found him camping just outside of town," Jack said. "He had a tent but hardly anything else. Let's just say that I don't think he thought this all the way through when he took off."

Dylan and Missy weren't the camping kind. I have no idea where he would have even procured a tent to sleep in. Maybe he borrowed it from a friend?

"I didn't poison Alvin," Dylan said when he and Missy finally broke apart. "I was in the kitchen because I was looking for Tedi. I wanted to ask her to watch over you while I was gone."

Missy pushed at his shoulder. "You shouldn't have gone anywhere."

Dylan hung his head. "I know that now. The minute I crossed the town line I knew that I'd made a mistake but I didn't know what else to do. It's all been so crazy."

"You're here now," Missy said. "That's the important thing. And you're even in a suit for the service."

"We stopped and let him get changed," Jack said.

Dylan squared his shoulders, taking a deep breath. "I love you, Missy. And I've done a lot of thinking about all of this. I think...I think we should just give it all away. The money, I mean. Maybe keep enough to buy a house and put some in trust for our kids' college but get rid of the rest. There are some really wonderful charities out there that could use our help."

Missy's smile grew wider and she clapped her hands together. "I am so glad you said that. It's what I was thinking too. We were already happy. We don't need all that money. I would love to help you give it all away."

They hugged again and I had to wipe a tear from my eye. They already had everything the needed. They didn't need a pile of cash to be happy.

"They're doing the right thing," I said softly to Jack who was standing next to me. "They don't need the money to be happy. They just need each other."

Jack's brows rose. "You almost sound like a romantic, Tedi."

"Maybe I'm softening in my old age."

He reached out and tucked a red curl behind my ear. "It looks good on you."

Jack could get mushy every now and then. I didn't mind.

"I'm glad they're giving all the money away. They'll be happier."

"You don't think that money can buy happiness?"

I didn't. It could buy a lot of things. Great medical care. A therapist. Healthy food and a warm home. And those things are important. But Missy and Dylan already had those things…minus the therapist.

"Money can buy peace of mind. But once you have enough what do you do with the rest? How many cars and houses could Missy and Dylan buy? How many five-star vacations could they take? At some point, a person doesn't need any more. Maybe I'm wrong. It just seems like they can keep a little and share a lot."

I must have said something very right because Jack was smiling as widely as Missy.

And that's weird, folks. Jack doesn't smile all that much.

"I'm glad to hear you say that, Tedi. It's time to go to the service. Are you ready?"

"I am. Are you?"

He patted his pocket where he'd tucked his cell phone.

"I am. Hopefully, I'll get a call from the lab today before everyone leaves after the reception."

Right. The still unsolved murder. We'd been sidetracked a bit. Time to get back to the case.

Who killed Vivian? And did the same person try and kill Alvin?

And an even better question…

Would they be at the funeral service today?

Chapter Fourteen

THE SERVICE WAS quite lovely. Dylan's father stood up and made a small speech as well as Alvin. Herschel and Bandy sat in the corner scowling and making everyone around them uncomfortable. Dylan and Missy sat next to his parents and held hands through all of it. There were a few tears, and some funny stories about the old days. Alvin mentioned that there would be a second small service in New York City for Vivian's friends and that everyone here today was invited to that too.

When it was over everyone mingled, nibbling at the buffet and crowding at the bar. Unlike the wedding reception a few days ago, however, this wasn't a party anyone wanted to linger at. The hall emptied within an hour, leaving just the close family and a couple of friends milling around.

"Tedi, I'm so sorry," Missy said, holding an empty glass and dabbing at a wet spot on the floor with a few cocktail napkins. "I spilled my drink."

"I'll grab a roll of paper towels," I said, heading off to the supply closet. "Don't worry about it."

I flipped on the single light in the closet, which was really just a small room with a bunch of metal shelves. I had to go all the way to the back to find the paper towels, sitting next to a huge cache of two-ply toilet paper. Nothing but the best for my guests.

As I was walking out, my knee hit the corner of a metal folding chair sitting too far out in the walkway, knocking over a leather messenger bag onto the floor and spilling its contents everywhere.

A few choice words came out of my mouth but I knelt down to pick it up, not sure what it was doing there to begin with. The metal chairs were usually stored in the coat room.

I recognized the bag as belonging to Andrea and that made perfect sense. She'd probably shoved it in here out of the way knowing that few people would come in here. Gathering the scattered papers, I noticed that one stack was thicker than the rest and looked a little worse for wear. The top page was titled *A Blushing Wind* and had Andrea's name on it.

It looked like a manuscript.

"What are you doing? Are you snooping in my bag?"

Andrea's voice came from the doorway, and like the whirlwind that she was, she was instantly next to me, pushing me out of the way and picking up the spilled papers and shoving them willy-nilly into the bag.

"I shouldn't have left it in here," she said, her tone brusque. "This isn't any of your business."

"I knocked it off the chair. I wasn't looking in your bag. I swear."

I had the distinct feeling she didn't believe me. She was muttering to herself, rummaging through the bag, clearly looking for something.

Maybe the thing in my hand?

"Are you looking for this?"

Andrea looked at the manuscript in my hand, the blood draining from her face. She'd looked annoyed a second ago, but now I couldn't quite figure out her emotions. She looked scared, furious, sad, and...something else I couldn't put my finger on. Determined, maybe?

She snatched the manuscript from my hand and crammed it back into the leather bag before straightening and slinging it over her shoulder. I stood as well, picking up the roll of paper towels that had been my original errand.

Her eyes narrowed, glittering with what I thought was anger. Her hand went protectively over the opening of the bag. "I guess you found what you were looking for. How long have you known?"

"Known?"

I had no clue what she was talking about.

"Don't play dumb. You found it. The manuscript. My book. *A Blushing Wind.*"

"I did, but I wasn't looking for it."

"I don't believe you. What tipped you off? How did you ever figure it out?"

It was like the two of us were having completely different conversations. But the hairs on the back of my neck were beginning to stand up, one by one. The little voice inside of my head was now screaming in my ear that Andrea was acting mighty suspicious. The other woman's cheeks were now bright red, her eyes hard and cold. She looked far from the happy and bustling event planner I'd known over the last couple of days. She looked...capable of murder.

So what exactly did I know?

"You're a writer too? Like Vivian."

"I am a writer. I'm a published author. Not that anyone knows that."

Her tone was bitter and I wasn't exactly sure why.

Something wasn't right.

"No one knows that you're published?"

"No one. She put her name on my book. She stole it."

My brain was going a mile a minute, trying to put what she was saying together. I had an inkling now...

"Vivian stole your book?"

"Alvin gave her my book to read," Andrea spat out. "He asked her to give me some feedback on my work. Instead she stole it and published it as her own."

Wait...Alvin? And Vivian had stolen the book? It was all becoming clear now.

"Is that why you killed her?"

Andrea would have had full run of the convention center. No one would have questioned her actions. Plus, no one had any idea she had any motive.

"When I talked to her about giving me the credit, she

laughed. She *laughed* at me. I knew I had to do something."

"What did Alvin say?"

"He said that we would talk to her here. That we would make her understand that I didn't care about the money. I just wanted the credit. He'd make her see reason."

"And did he talk to her?"

Andrea sniffled, a lone tear streaking down her cheek. "She said that she didn't care. That she couldn't tell anyone that she didn't write it. She told us that she'd give us some of the money but I wasn't going to stand for that. I was going to get what was rightfully mine."

This was bad. So very bad.

"So you confronted her at the reception?"

"I did. She laughed again. She told me that I was lucky that I was published at all. She said that I should be *grateful*. That people were reading what I'd written. She left to go into the coatroom to take a call. I was so angry. I was shaking. I went after her. I didn't even realize what I was doing until it was done. I'd grabbed that bookend and hit her on the back of the head. I'm not sorry either. She deserved it."

Holy cow. I hadn't seen this coming.

"Then you came back to the reception and called for the bouquet toss to distract everyone. But you couldn't know that it would get out of hand and the door would be knocked open."

She nodded. "I thought I'd have more time, but it didn't matter. It was easy to put the blame on Herschel and Bandy. I wasn't lying when I said that they argued with Vivian earlier that day. It was the truth. They had motive. They hated Vivian."

"What about Alvin eating that strawberry?" I asked. Had that only been this morning? It seemed so far away. "Was that just an accident?"

"I was in the kitchen and took a couple of strawberries from one oatmeal bowl and put them in Alvin's. It was so easy. No one paid me any attention. Alvin knew that Vivian had stolen my book. So far he hadn't said anything, but I couldn't take the chance that he might tell the sheriff that I had a motive. I had no idea that Dylan would be in the kitchen as well."

"You couldn't possibly have known that Jack would order oatmeal with strawberries."

"That's true," she agreed. "But I knew that we were serving strawberries at the reception today. I made sure of it. That way they would be in the kitchen and it wouldn't look strange for me to be checking on them. The fact that the sheriff ordered them this morning was just my lucky day."

She and I had different definitions of luck.

"And you thought it would look like an accident?"

"That was the plan. I didn't expect him to carry an allergy pen around."

"How did you even know he had an allergy?"

"I heard him tell someone at a book club meeting. He turned down the strawberry shortcake."

I should have been paying more attention. I really should have been more alert, but my mind was whirling with all that I'd learned in the last five minutes. That's my only excuse.

Because Andrea had reached into that leather bag and pulled out a small handgun.

Well...this wasn't good. I didn't like guns in general and being on this end of one wasn't my happy place.

"Andrea, don't do anything rash."

Like shoot me. I had a lot to live for.

Puppies. Ice cream. Rainy days. My friends. My family. And...Jack too.

"You know about me. I can't let you ruin this."

"I don't want to ruin anything for you. I think it's terrible what Vivian did. I can understand how upset you would be."

I now understood Vivian's reluctance to cross over. I had a strong feeling she wasn't going...up.

"You'll tell your boyfriend and then I'll go to prison. I can't let you do that."

I opened my mouth to tell her that I wouldn't tell Jack but the words wouldn't come out. Even with a gun to my chest, I couldn't lie. Which was stupid. This was totally the time to tell a whopper and yet I couldn't say it.

I'm an idiot. Soon to be a dead one. I had sweat trickling down my back and my heart was racing faster than a car at Le Mans. I was terrified and I didn't want to die.

"There has to be another way, Andrea. If you kill me, Jack isn't going to rest until he finds out who did it. Then you will have killed two people. You'll definitely go to prison for two murders. You can explain about Vivian. A jury would under-stand. But me? That's just cold-blooded murder. They'll put you away for the rest of your life for that."

I could see her waver at that moment. She didn't want to go to prison and I didn't want to die. We were at a stalemate. She wasn't quite ready to pull the trigger and I didn't want her to. Where did we go from here? We weren't going to waltz out of the supply closet best buddies, pretending that nothing happened.

My fingers reflexively tightened on the paper towels and for a moment it crossed my mind to throw them at her. Just for the distraction. I only needed a second to get a running start. But then I measured the distance between me and the door and with her in between, there was no way I was going to make it out alive.

A creaking sound captured my attention and she and I both looked up to see a tall set of shelves swaying back and forth as if there was an earthquake or maybe a tornado. Except that the other shelves were fine. It was just that one.

Andrea had turned, the arm with the gun dropping down, but I never got the chance to make a break for it. The metal shelves creaked again loudly and swayed again, this time falling toward Andrea. She loudly screamed as an avalanche of cleaning products and boxes fell on top of her, the gun skidding away harmlessly.

And me? I stood there in complete shock at the scene before me. I'd almost died but was saved at the last minute. Again.

Shelves don't usually just fall over all by themselves. These were no exception. Edward was standing there, his arms crossed over his chest, his expression resolute.

"You saved my life."

"She killed Vivian."

That was all we said to each other before Jack ran in, surveying the carnage of what was once my supply closet.

"Are you okay, Tedi?"

"I am. Andrea did it."

"I know. Her fingerprints were on the bookend plus a feather from Andrea's sweater was found smeared in the blood."

Those feathers. They'd been distinctive and now they were going to be evidence against her.

Vivian's killer had been caught. Missy and Dylan could go on their honeymoon.

And me? I could finally breathe again.

Maybe I really should leave all of this investigation stuff to Jack. If I were a cat with nine lives I'd be extremely worried about now.

THE NEXT MORNING Daisy and I were sitting in a booth at the Grateful Raven having breakfast – waffles for me and a yogurt parfait for her – when she pointed out the window toward the sheriff's station.

"Looks like the county is picking up Andrea."

Since this was a small town, Jack didn't have the facilities to house long-term prisoners. It might be months before the trial took place.

Jack was standing on the sidewalk with Andrea, handcuffed and unsmiling, as she was loaded into an SUV. He said a few words to the other officer and then they pulled away. He turned and looked straight at me, which at one time would have creeped me out but now I took it in stride. He had powers and for all I knew he could probably feel me watching. He did surprise me, however, by walking into the diner and sitting down next to me. A waitress immediately filled a coffee cup for him. They knew him well.

"So it's over," Daisy said with a sigh. "You must be relieved, Jack."

"I am, although it's always hard to see someone face serious justice like this. She's looking at a lot of years behind bars. One murder and one attempted as well."

"She did kill someone," Daisy replied, her gaze lingering on the sidewalk where Andrea had been standing. "Even if it was for a good reason. Or what she thought was a good one. Did Vivian even say she was sorry when you told her?"

That meeting had been a mess. Jack and I had gone to Grandma Lane's home to tell Vivian, Edward in tow. When Jack had informed her that she'd been killed by Andrea because she'd stolen the manuscript and made everyone believe it was hers, she hadn't seemed all that upset. Or sorry. Or remorseful. If anything, she was concerned that Andrea would go to the press and tell the world that Vivian hadn't written that last book.

And that was totally going to happen because Andrea was

determined that she get the credit for writing the book even if she had to go to prison for doing it.

"Not really," I said, taking a sip of my coffee. Caffeinated goodness. "She said that she had *no choice* as she was up against a deadline and she had terrible writer's block. When Alvin handed her Andrea's manuscript for Vivian to read, she said it was a sign that it was for her. She didn't really seem to care about Andrea's feelings. She just said that Andrea could write another book."

"She was completely cold about it," Jack said bluntly. "Classic narcissist. It was all about her and she didn't care about anyone else."

Daisy shook her head. "How are Missy and Dylan taking it?"

That was the only good news in all of this.

"They left on their honeymoon last night. They'll be traveling around Italy and Greece for the next two weeks."

I was happy that I'd managed to get to hug both of them before they left for the airport. They deserved some peace and happiness after the whole wedding fiasco.

Daisy took the last bite of her parfait. "So did Vivian cross over then?"

Jack and I exchanged a glance. He didn't respond, leaving it up to me.

"Actually...no. Edward was there as well. When she wasn't sorry about stealing Andrea's manuscript Lane started to get upset, telling Vivian that she couldn't be friends with a liar and a thief. Edward got upset as well and grabbed Vivian's hand. Next thing we knew they just vanished. Poof. Gone."

Daisy looked around the diner. "Are they just invisible? Maybe they're hanging around town."

Jack shook his head. "I felt them leave. They're definitely out of Ravenmist. I do think that Edward is going to be surprised though about how much less energy he's going to have outside this town."

I hadn't thought about that. Without Jack in the near vicinity giving off massive quantities of demon energy, a spirit like Edward would need to be careful and conserve. A brand-new ghost like Vivian would hardly have any at all.

"Does Missy know?" Daisy asked quietly. "Is she upset?"

I shook my head. "I told her. I think she's sort of sad but she's fine. She wants Edward to be happy."

I'd also told Terrence and he'd taken the news well. He had said that he thought Edward would end up back in Ravenmist at some point in the future. He might be right. This was all Edward had known for decades.

Terrence had also volunteered to help Missy out at the bookstore, doing the tasks that Edward used to handle. He was there right now, opening the store for the day.

"Another murder all sewn up," Daisy stated. "Now we just need to figure out how to use the bowl that we found and how time travel might be able to help us against all the evil demons."

"Maybe we could travel back in time to when Orien got his power," I joked. "And stop it from happening. That might help us out."

No one said anything. Silence. Jack and Daisy were staring at me. The whole situation had turned incredibly awkward.

"What? What did I say?"

It must have been something stupid. Right?

I hope you enjoyed Wedding Bell Boos! Don't miss the next mystery in the Ravenmist Whodunit series.
Thank you for reading.

Don't miss a thing! Sign up to be notified of Olivia's new releases:

Mailing List: eepurl.com/gdVe3T

About The Author

Olivia Jaymes is a wife, mother, lover of sexy romance and cozy mysteries, and caffeine addict. She lives with her husband, son, and two spoiled dogs in central Florida and spends her days typing on her computer with a canine on her lap.

She is currently working on a new cozy mystery series – *A Ravenmist Whodunit* – in addition to her other ongoing romance series.

Visit Olivia Jaymes at

www.OliviaJaymes.com